A KILLING TRUTH

A Leine Basso Thriller Prequel

D.V. BERKOM

Cover by Deranged Doctor Design

ISBN: 0692659617
ISBN-13: 978-0692659618

For Mark

CHAPTER 1

October 2006—Eastern Europe

LEINE CHECKED HER watch as she waited for the target to emerge from the concrete block building. Practical as only Soviet-style architecture could be, nevertheless the crumbling façade gave the impression of faded power, like a once-famous tenor now down on his luck and sucking on throat lozenges in order to save his voice.

She'd wait five minutes longer and then leave if Igor Glushenko didn't show. There was no sense freezing her ass if her quarry decided to take his time with his mistress. Besides, she wasn't completely on board with Eric's instructions. There were other, less intrusive ways to fulfill the contract, and it made her wonder why her boss had chosen her for the job.

The cool air was damp from the recent squall that had just blown through the ancient city, the resultant mist hiding a few of the cars below her as though an unseen hand had intentionally obscured the block for effect. She glanced through the rifle sight once more and made a minor correction.

Ah, the glamorous life of a jet-setting assassin.

Leine inhaled and released her breath slowly, watching the condensation evaporate in the air before her.

And waited.

She didn't enjoy this part of her work. Leine had fought her impulsive and impatient nature all her life. But the extraordinary self-discipline she'd gained as a result had made her one of the best in her field. The majority of her colleagues went for the expedient solution, never considering the far-reaching implications of their choices, like political fallout and instability. They preferred to leave those problems to the higher ups. Leine thought through every action, treating each job like a chess match she was determined to win. By staying several steps ahead of her competition, she minimized blowback.

But with notoriety came frustration. Although her services were in demand, jobs had become more complicated and she found herself entering a gray area where the result wasn't necessarily what it seemed. Before, she'd been able to justify her actions without an assassin's guilt keeping her awake. Yes, she killed for a living, but her targets were the lowest of the low. She used to eliminate criminals who, if allowed to continue, would gladly take down the United States and her allies, or kill innocents in their quest for power.

And now? Now she questioned the direction her boss, Eric, was taking the Agency, whether the motivation for her assignments had more to do with greed.

The hair on her neck prickled her skin and she scanned the surrounding rooftops, making sure she was alone.

Just then, the front door to the building across the street opened. Wearing an expensive leather coat, a heavyset bear of a man emerged, flanked by two armed gunmen. After a brief reconnaissance of the block, they headed for a black SUV parked at the curb. The target was smiling. Clearly, he'd had a good session with his mistress.

Igor Glushenko will die a happy man today.

"Target in sight," she said into her mic, her voice low.

"Copy that," came the reply.

Leine dropped her head, the sniper rifle snug against her shoulder, and sighted in for the shot. A woman wearing a long skirt with her shirt unbuttoned to her navel appeared in the doorway, waving what looked like a silk cravat. The target turned and smiled. Leine's finger rested lightly on the trigger as she tracked Glushenko through the scope.

"Dammit," she muttered.

"Problem?" her handler, Lou, asked.

"The mistress. I'm going to wait to take the shot." The fewer witnesses, the better.

"Your call," Lou answered.

Glushenko's grin could only be described as licentious as he grabbed the woman around the waist with one arm and pawed at her breasts with his free hand. The woman's giggles were loud enough to reach Leine's ears.

C'mon, already. Go back inside, but leave Glushenko.

She'd been tempted to call off the job. Nothing had felt right from the start. From Eric's unusual request that she set up on a rooftop across the street from where the Russian's mistress lived—Leine preferred to work in a

3

less conventional manner to keep the target's security off guard—to the directive to use a rifle to take Glushenko out. Normally weapons were the operative's choice.

Glushenko's security detail, two tall, muscle-bound men wearing tailored black suits and carrying machine guns, looked on with wide grins. The driver's door of the SUV opened and a man wearing expensive-looking aviator sunglasses emerged, his annoyance apparent by his deep frown. He gestured to one of Glushenko's security guards, who nudged the other, nodding toward the two lovebirds.

While the guard attempted to speed their farewell, the driver turned and scanned the rooftops. He appeared to hesitate near the spot Leine had set up and she froze. She was certain he couldn't see her, but the earlier unease she'd been feeling had her spooked. He cocked his head to the side like a golden retriever being told something it didn't understand, then raised his hand and said something into his sleeve. A second later he started toward the front door of the building below her. She keyed the mic, sending a signal to both Lou and Carlos that she needed a diversion, and quickly scanned the neighboring rooftops again.

As though on cue, Carlos rounded the corner with his head down, bouncing along with his iPod, earbud wires sprouting like anemic spaghetti from his ears. Immediately on point, Glushenko's men reached for their weapons.

Mid-street, the driver turned to assess the intruder. As Carlos came closer, the guards stepped in front of him, barring his way. Carlos looked up, surprise on his face, working the I-didn't-see-you angle. One of Glushenko's men pushed him and barked an order. The driver said something into his sleeve again, then turned and headed toward the group on the sidewalk.

Leine slid backward, taking the rifle with her. When she was far enough away that she could stand and not be seen from the street, she closed the lens covers on the scope, collapsed the rifle's bipod, and broke down the gun so it would fit in her duffle bag. She then quietly opened the door to the stairwell and descended.

When she reached the metal door leading outside she removed her ear mic and paused to listen.

Nothing.

She dropped the mic into her bag and opened the door to check for passersby. Not seeing anyone, she stepped into the alley and stopped to shift the duffel bag onto her shoulder.

The round hit the wall centimeters from her head. Bits of concrete sprayed her cheek. Leine dove inside the building as another bullet slammed into the metal door.

Sniper.

She scanned the area, searching for the best exit.

A door banged open at the front of the building, accompanied by the sound of footsteps pounding toward her.

Glushenko's men.

Heart racing, she scrambled to her feet and sprinted for the stairs, taking two at a time. At the first landing she paused to catch her breath. Four corridors radiated outward from the central staircase, each hallway consisting of a dozen or more apartments.

She continued up the staircase and veered onto floor five, taking the easternmost hallway, far from the sniper's position. Several recessed doors with apartment numbers stood on either side of the corridor. Two of the ceiling lights had burned out, leaving the area in partial shadow.

Cardboard covered a window at the end of the passage, a fast fix-it job to keep out the cold. Footsteps echoed up the staircase as her assailants closed in.

Leine slid the pistol from her holster, screwed on the suppressor, and shot out the remaining lights, plunging the hall into darkness. Letting the duffel bag fall to the floor, she crossed the now-dark hall, moving to a doorway several apartments closer to the window. She dropped to one knee in a modified crouch and pulled up the hood of her jacket. The black material matched her clothes, giving her a semblance of camouflage.

The footsteps stopped at her floor, followed by silence. Leine breathed in slowly and let it out, calming the adrenaline dump. She aimed the gun.

Steady.

Whispers drifted toward her as a shadow fell across the floor near the entrance to the hall, then slid from view. Two gunmen ghosted up the steps, heading for the next level. Seconds later there was a pop and the fifth floor landing grew dark.

Couldn't be the sniper. Not if he'd set up on an opposing roof. There hadn't been enough time. And she doubted it was Glushenko's driver. Someone had to stay back and protect the Russian.

A third gunman?

Leine waited.

A minute passed. And then another.

Then two more.

Still she waited. Motionless. Listening. She lost track of time.

There.

The third gunman shifted position. The sound was barely a whisper. Right side, near the hallway entrance.

It wouldn't be long.

Minutes later—two? ten?—the murky silhouette of a man's profile materialized at the end of the hallway as he peered around the corner. Leine tracked his movements, reining in her impatience.

His head swiveled in the gloom as he scanned the hallway, his gaze appearing to linger on the dark shape of the duffel bag. Leine remained still, finger on the trigger, the cramp in her right knee screaming at her to move.

The man eased around the corner, gun leading the way as he hugged the wall. Leine fired two rounds in rapid succession. The man's head snapped back and hit the wall with a thud, and his body slid to the floor. There was a brief pause, and then shouts and footsteps erupted on the floor above her, the echoes exploding down the stairwell.

Leine sprinted to the bag, picked it up, and raced to the window. She ripped the cardboard away and threw the duffel onto the fire escape before diving through the opening. Shots pinged off the metal railing, and she rolled to one side. She spun around and came up in a crouch, then glanced through the window.

Glushenko's bodyguards advanced toward her, one on each side of the hall. She emptied her gun into the hallway, and both men dove for cover. She got lucky and hit the larger one in the shoulder. Leine ducked behind the wall to reload. A spray of bullets erupted from their AK-47s, slamming into the concrete next to the window. Ejecting the spent mag, Leine jacked in a full one and waited for a pause in the action. Her back to the wall, she rotated and aimed through the window.

The second man went down, a bullet to the throat. Gun in his left hand, the larger one squeezed off a round, but it went wide. This time, Leine hit center mass and the big guy toppled to the floor. An apartment door cracked open, but quickly closed.

Five minutes later, Leine was in a taxi on her way to the hotel and her rendezvous with Carlos. She leaned her head back on the seat and took long, slow, deep breaths until her heart rate returned to normal.

The sniper in the alley had been waiting for her.

Her hand trembled from the residual adrenaline as she punched Lou's number into her phone.

"Hey, Lou, checking in."

"Took you a while," he answered. "Everything okay?"

"Yeah, there was a slight delay, but I'm almost to the hotel." She eyed the taxi driver, who glanced at her in the rearview mirror and then quickly looked away.

Leine didn't normally use a spotter, but Carlos had just finished a job in Italy and offered his services when she'd voiced her concerns about the target. He flew in the night before and they discussed the job over dinner. Whereas Carlos was ground support, Lou worked remotely, observing via satellite feed and the ubiquitous security cameras found all over Europe. Having ties to the US government did have its perks.

After a circuitous route designed to throw off even the most persistent tracker, the taxi driver dropped her at the door to the touristy hotel. She went up to her room, using the stairs once she was sure no one waited for her in the lobby. Before entering, she checked the "tell" she placed at the top of the door to see if someone had been inside the room in her absence. It was still intact. Once inside, she added extra security to the door by installing a portable lock.

The half-finished bottle of red wine on the desk beckoned. She poured herself a glass and sat in a chair near the bed.

Not only had there been a sniper covering her exit, but she was certain Glushenko's driver knew she was on the roof. If she hadn't stopped to shift the bag to her other shoulder, there was a good possibility she'd be dead. Clearly, she'd been compromised. But by whom?

Fifteen minutes and a glass and a half of wine later, three knocks followed by two more sounded at the door. Leine let Carlos in and secured the locks. He crossed the room, corralling the bottle and a clean glass before sliding the other chair next to hers to sit down. She took her seat as he divvied up the rest of the wine and raised his glass in a toast.

"To your instincts."

Leine touched her glass to his and took a drink. "You could say that." She recounted the events of the ambush.

Carlos leaned forward and checked her over. "You're all right?"

Leine nodded.

"Why didn't you call for help?"

"No time. I removed the comm." She sighed, took another drink. "Any ideas?" she asked.

"Could be you pissed someone off." He stared at the glass in his hand. "Could be Eric."

"Eric." Leine frowned. "You think he wants me dead?"

"I don't know. Maybe. It's an open secret we're together." Carlos grimaced. "Like I told you last night. Things are changing. And not for the better."

"You said you had proof of what he was doing. Where?"

"Storage locker on the ground floor of my building. The key's well hidden. Number nine."

Carlos had been collecting intelligence on the director of the clandestine agency for several months and was close to sending the incriminating evidence to Eric's superior, Scott Henderson.

9

"Are you sure you're not just making assumptions about his involvement?" If their boss wanted her dead because of her association with Carlos, then Carlos's claims of Eric's illicit dealings made sense.

Carlos nodded. "Pretty damn sure. I realize what we do is supposed to stay under the radar, but the jobs he's been taking on the side go way beyond that. Not what I signed up for." He finished his wine and stood.

Carlos and Leine, along with a select group of others, were considered elite black ops for an organization known simply as the Agency. The name similarity to the Central Intelligence Agency was intentional. A shadow organization of highly skilled assassins tasked with removing targets who threatened the United States or her allies, the organization's objectives were government sanctioned but strictly on a need-to-know basis. They rarely worked with the CIA or NSA, preferring to operate in a fluid environment that the operatives referred to as the Shadowland. Carlos believed that, along with actual jobs the Agency was legitimately tasked to do, Eric was using the group for illicit and mercenary purposes without their knowledge.

"We're not terrorists for hire," Carlos muttered. "Eric needs a refresher on the Mission Statement."

Leine drained the rest of her wine and set the glass on the nightstand. "Are you close to letting Henderson know?"

"Soon. One more sweep should do it." By sweep, Carlos meant hacking into Eric's personal computer to do one last scan of its contents.

"Just be careful to cover your tracks. You know Eric changes up his security settings—you don't want to be caught in one of his traps."

"I've got it handled. He won't suspect anything." Carlos gave her a slow, sexy smile, a shank of dark hair falling across his face. "Hungry?" he asked.

"Not for dinner."

With a wicked grin, Carlos met her on the bed. She pushed him onto his back and straddled his hips. Lifting her arms, she slid her shirt over her head and let it fall to the floor, then reached behind to unhook her bra. Desire flared in his eyes as Carlos helped remove her pants. Her passion rising, Leine tugged off his long sleeved T-shirt and tossed it aside, pausing long enough to pinch his nipples. Carlos inhaled sharply and slid his hands up her torso to encircle her breasts and return the favor. Searing need shot through her and she groaned. She leaned over and planted kisses along his collar bone, tickling his chest with her hair.

His growing interest obvious, Carlos flipped her onto her back and slid his pants off the rest of the way, freeing his erection. They came together in frenzied yearning, the uncertainty and danger of their lives spurring them on.

It wasn't long before Leine forgot about Eric and the questions surrounding Glushenko.

CHAPTER 2

November 2006—Lithuania

I LYA BLEW ON his hands to keep them warm while they waited for the general to inspect the merchandise. He never understood why his uncle always insisted on meeting their clients in the middle of nowhere with only a frigid tent and a small space heater for warmth. It wasn't as though they couldn't hold negotiations in a warmer climate like the Middle East or perhaps some small island nation in the Caribbean hungry for a cash infusion. Or, better yet, the larger arms conventions held throughout the world with all the flash of a Hollywood premiere and sexy models to chat up during his free time.

Hands clasped behind his back and dressed in the sharply creased military uniform of his small country, the sixtyish General Davi perused their offerings, lips together in barely suppressed excitement at the smorgasbord of imminent destruction in front of him. His two aides, dressed similarly but with far less bling on their uniforms, stood close by, side arms at the ready.

One held a leather briefcase. Two of the general's khaki-wearing grunts with AK-47s slung over their shoulders stood guard near the entrance. Outside the tent, two friends from Ilya's uncle's military days were keeping watch.

As Uncle Piotr had taught him, Ilya made sure to place the larger, more expensive weapons near the front of the display, with the less costly pieces at the back. They could always count on the general's lust for the latest and greatest, even if the new features were more for show than actual use. Uncle Piotr had correctly pegged the general as an early adopter, one who must have the newest technology in everything, especially weapons, and was happy to pay the exorbitant prices attached to being first in line.

The general nodded at one of the submachine guns on display. "May I?"

"Of course." Uncle Piotr stepped aside so that Ilya could assist Davi with the weapon.

The general's expression switched to one of surprise as he lifted the gun to his shoulder. "It is so light."

Ilya smiled, nodding. "The RK1700 is constructed almost completely of polymer, making it much lighter than a conventional submachine gun." He picked up a more traditional gun, similar in size, and handed it to Davi. The general weighed both and gave the conventional firearm back to Ilya.

"Tell me about this."

Ilya caught Piotr's eye and gave him a quick smirk before turning to Davi. This would be an easy sale. The only question would be how many and how soon.

"The RK1700 is a prototype Personal Defense Weapon, not yet on the market. Due to our contact at the manufacturer, we were able to procure the first iteration of this state-of-the-art game changer." When Uncle Piotr had offered a sizable bribe to the contact, he'd been more than willing to sell out his employer and steal the prototype.

Ilya continued. "Weighing only one-point-two kilograms empty, the 1700 has a magazine capacity of fifty rounds, fully ten more than other competing PDWs on the market." As his uncle had instructed earlier, he paused to give the general a moment to absorb the information. Piotr gave him a quick, proud smile. Ilya nodded at the compact weapon. "As you can see, the smaller size will work well in close quarters. It uses a short stroke piston gas system, much like the MP7, and has better accuracy."

The general sighted along the barrel, tracking an imaginary quarry, then returned the weapon to the display table. "But why would I take a chance on this untried Russian technology when I am able to purchase the German-made PF-2100 at a fraction of the price?"

Ilya glanced at his uncle for help. Usually the general didn't balk at this stage of the negotiations. Piotr cleared his throat and stepped forward.

"I was unaware the Germans had opened up production of the PF-2100."

General Davi smiled and rocked forward on his toes, obviously pleased to possess inside information. "They have for my new broker. In fact, he has offered me quite a deal if I purchase directly through him."

This wasn't good. The general was one of their best customers, representing at minimum fifty percent of their business.

"I can match his offer." Uncle Piotr wasn't about to let Davi flounce off to another dealer without a fight.

General Davi remained silent, apparently weighing his options, and then said, "I'm sorry, but I have an agreement—"

"Does our history mean nothing to you?" Piotr asked.

Ilya detected barely suppressed anger in his uncle's usually calm voice. Ignoring the cold sweat trickling down his back, Ilya stepped forward, breaking the stare down between the two men.

"We do have something that I am certain your new broker does not," he said, defying his uncle's warning glance as he moved toward an empty table at the back of the tent. He reached under the table and brought out a stainless steel case.

"Ilya, I don't think the general is interested in this—"

But the general had perked up considerably and was already walking toward Ilya. His aides followed him, curiosity sparking in their eyes.

Uncle Piotr sighed and joined them. He leaned in close and whispered, "What the hell are you doing, Ilya? These have already been sold."

"Do you want to lose him?" Ilya whispered back. "Tell him we're taking orders."

"Gentlemen." Ilya made a point to look around the tent, as though checking to make sure no one else was nearby. Stupid, he knew, since they were out in the middle of nowhere, but if he had learned one thing from his uncle, it was that an effective sales pitch required at least an element of theater.

"Have you ever heard of NUCLEUS?" he asked.

"Yes, of course," the general answered, irritation lacing his voice.

"Then you know their work is considered proprietary by the United States government, and that only a precious few multinational companies are allowed access to their data."

General Davi nodded, his attention riveted on the case.

Ilya continued. "For the past five years, my uncle and I have cultivated a member within this organization. A member who until recently had been understandably wary of our overtures."

Uncle Piotr took over the narrative. "Due to a shift in his circumstances, he is willing to work with us, as long as the money is sufficient and if we are careful with whom we share these secrets."

"I'm listening," the general said.

Ilya moved to unlock the case, but Uncle Piotr motioned for him to stop. General Davi frowned, clearly annoyed. *Don't provoke him too much, Uncle,* Ilya prayed. The general was known for his short fuse and impatience, especially when it came to weapons. Rumor had it he'd killed a man who took too long to load the magazine of a gun he wanted to use.

"Before I allow my nephew to show you what is in that case, I need assurances that you will continue to call on our services first before purchasing elsewhere."

Ilya watched the general closely, looking for signs that he was considering his uncle's request. Davi remained inscrutable.

"All I ask is that you give us first chance to win your business," Piotr added.

"Done." Davi waved his hand, dismissing Piotr's concerns. "What is this weapon that is so amazing?"

Uncle Piotr smiled and nodded at Ilya to open the case. Nestled in protective gray foam were three four-inch rounds, with an additional round split open to reveal the interior. A thin booklet, stamped *Top Secret* next to the company's logo, lay next to the open round.

General Davi stared at the case. "Bullets? Why would I need this? I have already more than enough stockpiled in my warehouses."

"Not like these you haven't." Uncle Piotr selected one of the brass-jacketed projectiles and held it up. "Meet the first small arms smart bullet."

Davi narrowed his eyes. "Am I to believe this actually works?"

"Yes."

The general shook his head and laughed. "My dear Piotr, don't be offended, but there has been talk of a so-called smart bullet since the seventies. So far, none have lived up to their promise."

Ilya slid the case closer to the general. "This one does. There is a tiny computer chip embedded inside the casing."

"A counterweight has been placed near its nose, much like a rocket, and the fixed fins near the tail keep its trajectory true," added Piotr. "Optical sensors have been placed near the head."

Davi leaned closer to inspect the interior view of the round.

Ilya continued. "We've done field trials. It's the most accurate bullet either of us has ever fired, and will course-correct for up to twenty-five hundred meters."

"Two and a half kilometers?" The general's mouth popped open in surprise. His aides glanced at each other, obviously impressed. Davi nodded at the aide with the briefcase. "This could make an assassin out of my secretary. I'll take as many as you can produce. How much?"

While Uncle Piotr and the general haggled over price, Ilya returned the 50-caliber round to the case. When the general's aide opened his briefcase, Ilya forced himself not to stare. He'd never seen that much money in one place before—all of it US currency.

Ilya glanced up at a muffled thud on the outside of the tent. A succession of cracking sounds erupted near the entrance. Both of the general's guards staggered backward and crumpled to the ground. Stunned, Ilya froze before his brain kicked into gear. He yelled a warning to his uncle as he slammed the case closed and dropped to the ground under the table. Frantic, he reached for his side arm. His spirits plunged with the memory of the general's insistence that he hand over the weapon to his uncle when the meeting started.

This can't be the general's doing—I saw his guards fall.

More shots cracked. Closer, this time. Three more bodies thudded to the ground. Ilya stayed where he was, his breath coming in short gasps as he fought through panic. Fear bloomed in his chest, magnifying his thundering heartbeat as he muttered a prayer for survival.

There were only three shots. Maybe the gunman has spared Uncle Piotr. Ilya remained on the ground, too scared to look, warmth spreading through his crotch as he pissed himself.

"What are you doing?" The general's outrage was belied by the slight waver in his voice.

Three shots, three bodies, and the general is still alive. The gunman has killed Uncle Piotr. Ilya craned his neck, trying to see under the edge of the tablecloth. His uncle's body was nowhere to be seen. A pair of legs appeared in Ilya's view—camouflage pants tucked inside tall boots.

"I'll take that, General."

The thick accent sent a chill careening down Ilya's spine. *How did the Frenchman know about this meeting?* If anything, only a handful of people knew of his uncle's extracurricular activities. If this man was actually the feared arms dealer known as the Frenchman, then the smart bullets were most certainly lost and Ilya and the general would soon be dead.

He could only guess what had happened to Uncle Piotr's men—two old military buddies who were supposed to be outside the tent monitoring the surrounding farmland for intruders.

"I was going to tell you about this as soon as we spoke again." General Davi's voice faltered and he paused. "Wait—where is the other case?"

Ilya shrank back, clutching the prized bullets to his chest. He needed to escape, burrow beneath the tent's wall, run for his life. But his legs wouldn't move. Helplessness overwhelmed him, and he fought back tears.

The man with the French accent sighed, reached down, and raised the tablecloth. Ilya squeezed his eyes shut, strangling the case with his hands.

"Get up. Now." The Frenchman's command brooked no argument. Hot tears coursed down Ilya's cheeks as he scrambled to his feet.

"Don't shoot me," he pleaded, angry with himself for having given up his side arm. He hadn't thought anything of the general's request at the time—not with his uncle's friends keeping watch outside. The Frenchman held out his hand and wiggled his fingers, dark eyes snapping with amusement. His narrow face and dark goatee reminded Ilya of the devil.

A shudder surged through him at the thought.

Reluctantly, Ilya put the case on top of the table and slid it toward him. The Frenchman opened the locks and, eyebrow arched, scanned the interior. Satisfied, he snapped the lid closed and put the case under his arm. The briefcase with the general's money was in his free hand. He then waved the general over to stand next to Ilya.

To his credit, Davi looked more angry than afraid but did as he was told. Ilya took solace in the general's show of apparent bravery and willed his tears away. If he was to die, then he would die well.

The Frenchman raised his weapon. Heart hammering in his ears, Ilya squeezed his eyes shut. The general sucked in his breath.

The Frenchman fired.

For a moment, Ilya thought he might already be dead, but then the general slumped to the ground beside him. When the second bullet didn't come, Ilya opened his eyes to slits. The Frenchman was perusing the other weapons.

None of them were loaded, or Ilya would have attempted to assassinate him. The Frenchman was the scourge of Russian arms dealers everywhere—a menace to be eradicated. No one was immune from the man's reach. He operated by his own impenetrable code, which included stealing and murder if it suited his needs. Ilya would have been a hero.

As if sensing his thoughts, the Frenchman turned to look at him. His piercing black eyes noted everything, like a predator on the hunt. At least, so Ilya imagined.

"You're wondering why I didn't kill you," he said, his tone conversational.

Ilya shook his head. He found it hard to speak. He spotted Uncle Piotr's lifeless body a few yards away on the floor and started to shake.

The Frenchman smiled, stepped closer. "Tell everyone you know what happened here today."

A giant of a man carrying a submachine gun pushed a hand truck through the entrance past the guard's bodies. The Frenchman acknowledged him and turned his attention back to Ilya.

"Tell them it is pointless to resist, as I will continue to gain control by any means necessary."

The giant began putting the weapons back into their cases and stacking them on top of each other on the hand truck.

Ilya finally found his voice. "Why did you kill my uncle?" The reality of his loss had begun to sink in.

The Frenchman smiled. "Because that's the only currency your kind understands." With that, he turned and left.

His knees suddenly weak, Ilya gripped the table for support. How would he explain this to his aunt and his mother, or even worse, Piotr's brother, Uncle Vladimir? He watched his uncle's blood seep onto the ground from the bullet wound to his head.

A quiet rage burned in Ilya Kovshevnikov's chest.

CHAPTER 3

November 2006—San Francisco, California

THREE DAYS LATER, Leine completed the Glushenko job—her way—and flew back home to Northern California, her misgivings about continuing to work for Eric at the forefront of her mind.

What the hell was she going to do? It wasn't like she could put "former assassin" on a résumé.

Too many years ago Eric had found Leine at a gun range near her home in San Diego, shortly after her father was killed during a covert operation for the army. At sixteen, she was an expert markswoman thanks to her father's insistence she become proficient with every kind of firearm available. She also had a firm working knowledge of hand-to-hand combat and could hold her own in a brawl with aggressors twice her size.

In addition to the barely suppressed rage that burned inside of her from losing both parents at a young age—her mother had died of cancer two years earlier—Leine had the practical skills Eric liked to see in his recruits. She basked in his attention and lavish praise and was soon his protégé at the Agency.

If Leine quit the Agency now, she'd have to freelance. Working as an assassin for hire for anyone who came along didn't suit her, and she was loath to make abrupt changes in her life. She had a teenage daughter to care for, and resigning would change their lives. They'd have to leave their peaceful, albeit expensive, home on the vineyard near the foothills of Calistoga. The generous paycheck she received each month would be difficult to match elsewhere, no matter what kind of job she found.

Besides, she believed in what she did: take out the dirtbags of the world to make it a safer, saner, place. A kind of legacy to leave her daughter.

She pulled up outside of her friend Marta's deceptively plain house on the outskirts of Santa Rosa and parked. Marta and her husband, James, were her daughter's godparents, and they looked after her whenever Leine had to leave.

"Good to see you," Marta said when she answered the door. Leine walked inside and they embraced. Marta was from Spain and had met James when he'd been in Madrid studying architecture. They married and moved to California, where James was a partner in a local firm.

"April," Marta called up the stairs, "your mom's here." She smiled at Leine. "Can you stay a while? I know James would love to see you."

"Sorry, much as I'd like to, we need to get home," Leine said. April bounded down the stairs, two at a time, purple backpack in hand, her long auburn hair streaming behind her. Tall and slender, she had a defiant look in her green eyes, reminding Leine of herself.

Damn, she looks more like me every day. Disconcerting, to say the least.

April gave Marta a hug goodbye. At five-nine she towered over the older woman. She glanced behind Leine. "Where's Carlos?"

"He's still overseas, but should be back tomorrow." Eric had given him a last-minute assignment, and instead of coming home with Leine he'd flown to an undisclosed location.

April's face fell and she let the backpack slide to the floor. "Darn. I wanted to talk to him about this really cool formula I learned in math."

Leine knew better than to suggest April talk to her. Not because Leine didn't understand math—she'd taken advanced calculus and trigonometry in her early days as a trainee for the Agency—but because April reserved certain discussions solely for Carlos.

"We'll see him this weekend."

April brightened. "We're going to the City? Awesome!"

They said their goodbyes and walked out to the car. The sun was just beginning its descent toward the horizon, casting everything in a dusky orange hue.

"Did you have a good time?" Leine asked.

April shrugged. "I guess."

Leine tried again. "Should we get pizza for dinner?"

Another noncommittal shrug.

She's angry with me again. What the hell did I do this time? Leine unlocked the doors and they both got in.

Keep trying, Leine. It's bound to work eventually, right?

At one time best friends, somewhere around the age of eleven Leine's relationship with April had taken a surly turn. More often than not, Leine found herself in what could only be described as enemy territory. Raising a daughter alone was enough of a challenge. This new quality to their relationship had Leine scratching her head and yearning for more jobs out of country.

"Look. I get it. You're unhappy with me. Is it because I was gone so long this time?" She peered at April, who was looking out the window at nothing in particular.

"Because, you know, if it is, there isn't much I can do about it right now. It's my job."

Giving up for the time being, Leine started the car and pulled away from the curb. They drove in silence along eucalyptus-and oak-lined streets, past older, upper-class homes dotting the perimeter of a golf course. Soon the scenery turned to expansive vineyards and quaint wineries, and they passed several bicyclists in brightly colored shorts and helmets. Thirty-five minutes later, they turned left onto Main Street and drove through the picturesque town of Calistoga, headed for home.

They pulled onto the gravel drive and made their way through the vineyard toward the house. The cabernet leaves had turned with the cooler temperatures, painting the landscape orange and yellow, with traces of deep red. Leine smiled at the welcome sight. She considered herself lucky to have found the private rental.

As they neared the two-story farmhouse, a shiny black Mercedes Benz could be seen parked in the circular drive.

"Is that Eric's car?" April asked, sitting up straight.

"Looks like it," Leine replied. *What is he doing here?*

She pulled into the detached garage and parked. April shot out of the car and ran for the house before Leine could shut off the engine. Leine gathered her things from the trunk and made her way toward the house. *This is what you get for insisting on raising April alone.*

Understandably, her daughter became attached to whichever man April happened to spend the most time around. For the first few years after she was born, Eric was a constant, showing up when Leine needed a break, bringing all sorts of amusing toys and games to pass the time. Soon, though, the newness wore off and Eric grew more distant, citing a heavy workload and added responsibilities. Though young, April had felt his absence acutely, assuming his abandonment had been her fault no matter how much Leine assured her it was not. Now, every time she saw him, she did her best to recapture his attention.

Maybe I can talk Carlos into moving up here. At least that way April would have the benefit of a more suitable male figure.

The irony of an assassin as a role model for a preteen was not lost on Leine.

She approached the wraparound porch to April's squeal of delight. The two of them sat on rattan chairs, a small blue box between them on the low glass table. She turned to show Leine what Eric had brought her.

"Isn't it beautiful, Mom?"

Leine eyed the diamond-and-topaz-encrusted tennis bracelet with a mixture of annoyance and trepidation. "It is that." She turned her attention to Eric. "What's the occasion?"

Eric smiled modestly and shrugged. "Do I need a reason to give a gift to my favorite girl?" April beamed as she held out her wrist so he could close the latch.

After so many years of knowing him, Leine found it easy to see through his boyish good looks and aw-shucks demeanor. He didn't do gifts without some kind of agenda attached. Now that Carlos had planted a seed of doubt in her mind, she was on high alert to any kind of undercurrent. She leveled her gaze at him, making it plain with a look what she thought of giving a twelve-year-old such an expensive gift. Eric averted his eyes and smiled at April, the tips of his ears turning pink.

"Can I wear it to school?" April asked Leine, happiness practically oozing from her pores.

"Probably not, honey. I think you should save this for special occasions."

April's face fell. "Can I at least show Cory and Alexa?"

"Sure. Why don't you invite them over?"

April perked up and gave Eric a hug. "Thank you, Eric. It's phat."

After she'd gone inside, Leine had a seat across from Eric.

"Now, Leine. I know what you're thinking, but this time it's really about April."

Leine scoffed. "Like all those times before, you mean?"

"Hey, give me a break." He leaned closer and lowered his voice. "I *am* her father. Just because we've been dancing around the subject for the last twelve years doesn't mean I can't have some kind of presence in her life."

Leine checked the angry response that sprang to her lips and took a deep breath to calm herself. Antagonizing him wouldn't do any good and might harm the tenuous goodwill they'd managed to achieve in the last few years. Eric could be vindictive, especially if he thought his authority was being questioned. *Careful, Leine. He knows everything about you.*

Everything.

"We both agreed telling April was not in her best interest. Besides, you lost the right to have any say in her upbringing when you distanced yourself from her all those years ago."

"That doesn't change the fact I am her biological parent." Something shifted behind his eyes.

"Where are you going with this, Eric?"

Eric shrugged. "Nowhere. I just think it's time I took a more active role in our daughter's life."

"Right. I don't think so." Leine glared at him. "Are you trying to piss me off? Because you're doing a bang-up job." *Easy, girl. He might be an asshole, but he's a dangerous one.*

Eric's expression morphed from belligerent to aw-shucks mode, and he put his hands up, obviously trying to placate her. "That isn't the main reason I'm here." He cast a quick glance at the doorway before he leaned forward, lowering his voice.

"You've heard of Emile Robicheaux?"

"The Frenchman."

Eric nodded. "Turns out, he's been rather active. And not in a neighborly way."

"He's an arms dealer," Leine said, her tone matter-of-fact. Eric wasn't usually quite this dense.

His smile held a hint of condescension. "Of course. But he's upsetting a delicate balance and our Russian counterparts have expressed an interest in removing him from the equation."

"You're serious." Leine didn't bother keeping the disbelief from her voice. "And you're telling me this because—?"

"I want you to take the package." Eric sat back in his chair. "Take the package" was Agency parlance for accepting a target. "Look. I know what you're thinking—"

Leine shook her head. "No, you don't. Why on earth would you send one of ours to do *their* dirty work?"

"Because he's got connections and would know they were after him, which will piss him off. You don't want to piss this guy off. My contact says he shows up at the smallest deal as long as there are weapons and cash, and then kills all but one witness. There's no way he could know about the meets unless he's using informants. At his last appearance he scored a smart bullet prototype that NUCLEUS was working on. Let's just say our boss is not pleased."

"How do you know the Russians are telling the truth? They could just be trolling for some sucker to take the gig, hope they get lucky."

"I've known my guy a long time. He's got a good track record. He asked me if the tables were turned, who would I put on it and I told him. I want it done right." Eric shrugged. "You're my best."

"I'm still not convinced." The Russians had numerous agents that could do what Eric was suggesting. There had to be more to the story.

There always was.

"It's a direct order."

Leine narrowed her eyes. "From whom?"

Eric pointed straight up. Obviously, he didn't mean God.

"You're telling me the vice president's involved."

"Came straight from Toby."

Toby acted as liaison between the vice president and Scott Henderson.

Leine couldn't argue that one. She couldn't ask to see the directive, since Henderson would never leave a trail— electronic or otherwise—especially if directed by the administration. Still, in light of the information Carlos had suggested he found, she wasn't comfortable taking Eric's word at face value. Memories of the problems with the Glushenko job flitted through her mind, reminding her she still didn't know who'd compromised the operation.

"That's all well and good, Eric, but I'm going to need more than just your word."

Eric's eyes narrowed. "Since when did you feel the need to question me?"

"Since I was almost killed on the Glushenko job."

He tilted his head in acknowledgement. "Fair enough. I admit I could have done more advance work."

"You think so?" Leine checked the sarcasm that sprang to her lips. She'd have to play along with him, keep him thinking she still trusted him. "Look, I understand the info on a target can be sketchy, but I'm convinced the ambush was the result of advance knowledge. Doesn't that give you pause?"

"The assailant could have gotten lucky."

"Lucky? A person steps off a curb and narrowly misses being hit by a bus. That's lucky. An ambush by four gunmen is a planned assassination."

"I disagree. There could be a number of explanations. Glushenko's a high-value target. I'm certain he routinely sets up advance security protocols wherever he goes. Even when he visits his mistress." He picked a piece of lint off his trousers. "You know the risks."

Let it go, Leine. There was no use arguing with Eric. She wanted to get a pulse on how he'd react, but he'd had too much time to practice his cover story. If he'd been involved.

"Fine. But I want a full dossier on the Frenchman. Whatever you've got, even if it's hearsay. I choose where, when, and how."

"Absolutely," he said, nodding. A moment of silence passed between them.

"Are we finished?"

Eric frowned, shifted in his chair. "Not quite. I have one more job for you to do before you go after Robicheaux."

"When?" Leine said, unable to keep the irritation out of her voice. "I'm already on April's shit list for being gone so long on the Glushenko job. Now you're sending me to do two jobs, back to back? You do remember April, right?"

Eric leaned forward and placed his hands on the table in front of him, his eyes glittering like hazel-colored diamonds. "You want to stay with the Agency, right?"

"Is that a threat?" Leine's face grew warm as a wave of anger rose in her chest. How long had she done exactly what he wanted? He admitted she was his best. Was he really so eager to have her leave?

Or dead?

His lips thinned with an insincere smile. "Of course not. More of a suggestion to appreciate what you have because of your career."

He leaned back and spread his arms wide, indicating their peaceful surroundings. Just then, a murmuration of starlings swooped down through the darkening night sky like a choreographed wave, landing as one in the recently harvested vineyard.

"Point taken." Leine didn't want to fight him. She wanted him to leave so she could go inside and be with her daughter. "When's my flight?"

"I'm waiting for intel. I should have the packet to you by next week. That way you can spend the weekend with April."

Leine stood and stared pointedly at Eric. He got to his feet.

"Say goodbye to her, will you?" he said, and walked down the porch steps to his car.

Leine waited until the Mercedes's taillights disappeared down the drive before she picked up the box and ribbon still on the table.

She wasn't looking forward to telling April she was about to leave town again.

Chapter 4

EMILE ROBICHEAUX CLOSED his eyes and brought the fifty-year-old scotch to his nose, detecting a hint of warm oak and rose. He took a small sip, swirled the liquid over his palate, sensing smooth caramel and a bite of orange. But wait—was that tobacco? Ah, yes. Perfection.

One could never go wrong with good scotch.

Oscar appeared in his periphery, a solid giant of a man whose mere presence signaled barely suppressed violence. Scars crisscrossed the large man's arms and neck, with one particularly angry-looking red welt searing his cheek from temple to just beneath his chin. Oscar had no illusions as to his appearance. Robicheaux had hired him to intimidate.

"What is it?" Robicheaux asked.

"There is news."

The Frenchman set the hand-blown glass on the table next to him and gave the giant his full attention.

"Glushenko has been assassinated."

Robicheaux nodded.

"Was it she?" Everyone in the arms community knew of the first attempt. Rumor suggested a woman assassin. They'd dubbed her *the Léopard*.

Oscar shrugged a massive shoulder. "There were no witnesses, but it's probable. The methods used on the others are similar."

The others Oscar referred to were several recent Russian assassinations, all well planned and successful. All attributed to the Léopard.

"Interesting." Robicheaux was intrigued. He'd known female assassins, of course, but never had there been one with this kind of reputation.

"There's more." Oscar shifted his feet, looking uncomfortable.

"Come now, Oscar. It can't be *that* bad."

Oscar met his gaze. "There's word of a contract. On you."

Robicheaux had been expecting this. He fully accepted the probability that one or another faction in the arms community would eventually call for his assassination. The question now was who?

"Let me guess. The Russians?"

"That's what's unusual. The request originated with them, but they've passed it on to someone else."

Robicheaux narrowed his eyes. "Who?"

"It's unclear. I've got someone working on it."

"Why would our paranoid friends hand someone else this prize?" Robicheaux sighed and picked up his glass. "My death would be cause for celebration throughout the Motherland."

"They believe you have an informant within their ranks."

"And they'd be correct." The Frenchman gazed at the amber liquid for a moment before taking a delicate sip.

"Keep me updated. I am interested in whoever it is that they trust with a contract of such import."

Oscar left him and he stared into the distance, lost in thought. As a rule, the Russians didn't farm out their wet work, preferring to extract every last bit of intelligence from the target first. It was possible this was an attempt to lure him into the open. Or, at the very least, expose his contact.

That would never happen.

CHAPTER 5

November—San Francisco, California

LEINE, CARLOS, AND April sat together on a bench near Fisherman's Wharf, picking apart a Dungeness crab. Seagulls swooped down, clumsy in their attempt to steal a section of the delicious appetizer for themselves, while Carlos gallantly waved them off. The three had walked the Embarcadero to the wharf under the sun-drenched, brilliant blue California sky. Along the way, Carlos teased April relentlessly, making them all laugh when she gave it back to him in spades. Like a family, Leine mused.

Nice.

When they were finished, April crumpled the leftover shells inside the wrapper and walked to a nearby garbage can, stopping to pet a woman's tiny dog on the way. Leine leaned her head back and closed her eyes, enjoying the warm sun on her face.

"Happy?" Carlos asked, joining her.

"Mmm. Very."

He lifted her hand and kissed each knuckle. She smiled.

"I want to marry you."

Leine opened her eyes and studied him. He leveled his dark gaze at her, and for a moment she found it difficult to remember what she wanted to say.

"I never pegged you as the marrying kind."

He grinned, slowly, and leaned in close. His breath tickled her cheek.

"I wasn't."

Leine inhaled deeply, losing herself in the subtle aftershave he wore just for her. Notes of citrus and exotic spice reminded her of their days in Morocco two years before. There was something to be said for marrying a man with a similar career. She wouldn't have to hide what she did for a living. The stirrings of desire curled through her, and she sank against him with a deep sigh.

"Get a room." April stood nearby with her hands on her hips in a mock display of disgust. Leine and Carlos laughed and reached for her, wrapping her in a giant hug that made her giggle.

Carlos glanced at his watch. "What do you say we pick up pizza and a movie and go back to my place?"

"Well, yeah," April said. "Can we get Harry Potter?"

Carlos rolled his eyes. "Well, yeah." He turned to Leine. "That all right with you?"

"As long as the pie's from Tony's."

An hour later, they were back at Carlos's apartment. The exposed brick walls and heating ducts worked with the elegance of the Turkish carpets and Mission-style furniture he favored, although the modern touches matched the hi-tech, open-concept kitchen. His floor-to-ceiling living room windows overlooked the Tenderloin District.

The Tenderloin, or TL to residents, had a long history of attracting colorful characters. Although known for its violent crime, Leine made certain April was always safe.

She also wanted her daughter to be familiar with different lifestyles in the belief that she'd grow into a less prejudiced human being. So far, it seemed to be working. April enjoyed chatting up the trannies outside of Divas and had made friends with several of them. Often, she put together bags of necessities to hand out to homeless people in the neighborhood.

After the movie and a quick game of Spades, April slipped off to bed, leaving Leine and Carlos alone on the couch with the last of a bottle of wine they'd opened for dinner. Leine leaned her head on his shoulder and looked out the window at the lights below them. In the corner, flames danced in the small fireplace.

"Do you ever think about leaving?" she asked. "Just giving up the life and finding something…different?"

"Like buying a vineyard and becoming a gentleman farmer?" Carlos nodded. "All the time. But then I remember what kind of money I make and that I'm damn good at what I do."

"Even after what you've learned about Eric?"

"Yeah." Carlos sighed. "I can't deny it's getting harder to justify the reasons. Owning a vineyard is starting to look awfully good." He shook his head and took a sip of wine.

Leine set her glass down and turned so she could look into his eyes.

"Are you going to tell me what you've found out, or are you waiting for the afterlife?"

"It's better if I don't. Plausible deniability."

"What, for me? Don't believe that for a second. I'm pretty sure knowing everything I can about what you've uncovered is a hell of a lot safer." She touched his face, and he kissed her palm.

"I can tell you this. Eric's employees are no longer exclusive to the Agency. He's running several of us as guns for hire, and the targets aren't always enemies of the United States."

"So you think Glushenko may be one of these extracurricular targets?"

Igor Glushenko had been a garden-variety small arms dealer with an illicit little side business going, but he hadn't done anything that would warrant a US-sanctioned assassination. At least, not that Leine could uncover through her sources. That kind of action generally required a substantiated threat to US interests. It was one of the reasons Leine was able to sleep at night.

"Not necessarily. I still think Eric could have ordered the hit to cover your death."

"But why? I've been with him since the beginning. He knows better than to think I'd be a threat."

"Because we're together." Carlos shrugged, and stared into his glass.

"And that matters because…"

"Think about it, Leine. You told me yourself you two used to have a thing—"

Leine scoffed. "That was over a decade ago."

Carlos put his hand up. "Hear me out. We both know how territorial Eric is, right?" Leine nodded. "Now that we're a couple, at a minimum he's going to be paranoid about our conversations. Who knows? Maybe he thinks we're planning to go out on our own. No doubt having me in the picture messes with his perception of control over you."

"Then why not try to eliminate you? Seems to me that would take care of his darkest fears." She couldn't keep the sarcasm from her voice. Somehow, she just didn't see Eric as a heartbroken, jilted ex-lover who didn't want anyone to have her.

Carlos shrugged. "How do we know he hasn't tried? Just because I'm still alive doesn't mean there hasn't been an attempt."

Leine narrowed her eyes. "What aren't you telling me?"

"Nothing." Carlos got up and walked to the wine rack. He chose another bottle and grabbed the opener and a small box off the counter before returning to the couch.

"You're deflecting. I know you too well, Carlos. What happened?"

"I'm just saying, worst case he's going to be freaked out because April has a new father figure in her life." He busied himself opening the bottle, ignoring her pointed look.

Damn him. Something had happened—she was sure of it—and he wasn't about to tell her.

"Have you at least taken precautions?" she asked.

Carlos smiled as he filled both glasses and set the bottle on the table. "What do you think?" he asked as he handed her the box. It was gaily wrapped with bright green ribbon. "For you."

Leine set her glass down and opened the gift. Inside was a sporty little multi-function timepiece with a chronometer, altimeter, clinometer, and compass, among other functions. She smiled and put it on. Leave it to Carlos to give such a thoughtful, practical gift.

"It's beautiful, Carlos. Thank you."

"There's one more thing." He reached inside the box and pulled out a smaller package wrapped in royal blue satin.

"What's the occasion?" she asked, taking it from him.

"No reason. I prefer giving gifts when the recipient doesn't expect it."

Leine carefully unwrapped the tiny package. "Oh. My," she breathed. A blue sapphire surrounded by brilliant diamonds in a platinum setting glittered in the firelight. She brought her gaze up to meet his. His eyes were dark with emotion.

"In case you didn't think I was serious earlier." He took the ring from the box and teased it onto her finger, kissing her palm.

"It's beautiful. Thank you." She trailed her hand across his jawline and down to his chest. The ring glowed in the deep orange firelight. Leaning closer, she whispered in his ear, "Don't think this will get you out of telling me why you think you've been targeted."

A chuckle emanated from deep inside him. "You, my love, are like a pit bull when you want something."

Ignoring the pit bull comment, Leine went on. "In Prague you mentioned you hid what you'd discovered about Eric in a storage locker in this building." She glanced around the apartment trying to determine where he would have hidden the key. The exposed brick walls held several possibilities, as did the plank wood flooring. "If what you're saying is true, then there may come a time when I'll need to access the information."

"You're asking me where the key is?"

"Yes." When he didn't reply, she rolled her eyes. "Jesus, Carlos. You asked me to marry you. Don't tell me you're going to be this secretive when we're husband and wife?"

Carlos raised his eyebrows. "Did you just accept my proposal?"

Leine smiled. "Maybe. If you tell me what happened to make you think Eric may have tried to kill you, then I'll certainly consider it."

"Let's not talk about that right now." Carlos leaned back and nuzzled her neck. "Right now I want to ravish you."

At first she resisted, but then thought better of it and relaxed into his embrace. A chill spiraled down her spine, igniting her senses. Matching his passion with her own, her hunger grew, and she soon lost focus. All that mattered was heated flesh searing heated flesh, hard matching soft, their inflamed desire rising in a frenzied, ancient dance.

Life is uncertain, Leine. Enjoy the moment.

She hoped there would be many, many more.

CHAPTER 6

THE NEXT MORNING, Leine awoke to warm sun filtering through sheer curtains. She didn't have to turn her head to know Carlos was no longer beside her. She listened to the early morning sounds of the street below as the aroma of freshly brewed coffee wafted in from the kitchen.

Content, she stretched her arms above her head and smiled as she looked around her. The bedroom reflected his personality—a stark white comforter and khaki sheets covered the bed, with soft blue paint on the uncluttered walls. Ice-white curtains draped from the ceiling to puddle on the floor in front of large windows, creating a vivid contrast with a lyrical painting he'd chosen by a contemporary Chinese artist.

She remembered the day he bought it. She'd met him in Hong Kong after a job, and they'd spent several hours scouring the city for art. On the last day, they stumbled upon a tiny gallery a few blocks from the waterfront, and Carlos had fallen in love with the painting, surprising her with his strong aesthetics.

She loved that he continued to surprise her.

Leine held out her hand and admired the sapphire and diamond ring. A perfect size, the piece made a quiet statement, in contrast to other engagement rings she'd noticed that she could only describe as gauche. She'd never been much for diamonds or precious stones and especially not gold. Carlos's choice showed that he had been aware of her preference for subtlety. All of which didn't really matter, since she'd never wear it in the field, and they rarely went out.

Carlos walked into the room clad only in a towel, accentuating his well-defined abs. Leine smiled and emitted a low growl as he handed her a steaming cup of coffee.

"April's still asleep," he said and sat on the edge of the bed.

Leine glanced at the clock on the nightstand. 6:30.

"Not for long." Her daughter hadn't yet started the typical teenage habit of staying up late and sleeping until noon.

"It's just as well. I've got an early flight."

"April's going to be disappointed." She knew better than to ask him where he was going. One of the tenets of their jobs was that they had to be ready to leave at a moment's notice and not disclose the location.

Carlos nodded. "Tell the little shit that while I'm gone I'll be thinking up ways to torture her."

Leine smiled. "She'll be ecstatic."

Carlos leaned in to give her a penetrating kiss but was the first to break contact. He rose and walked to the closet, where he pulled out a small flight bag which he began to pack.

"Anything wrong?" Leine asked. He was usually more playful in the mornings.

His back to her, he shook his head. "Not particularly." He continued packing. "Last night you asked about the key to the storage locker."

"What about it?" She threw off the covers and reached for her clothes, still on the floor where she left them.

"It's over there." He nodded toward the wall next to her.

Leine pulled her shirt over her head, and followed his gaze. "You mean behind the painting?"

"Yep."

Leine walked to the artwork and lifted it away from the wall, smoothing her hand along the exposed brick. Her fingertips slid over a subtle depression, next to the screw for hanging the picture. Noticing a hairline gap between the brick and mortar, she grasped the screw and wiggled the brick back and forth until it came free. It looked remarkably similar to the others. There didn't appear to be an opening. She looked over her shoulder at Carlos and raised an eyebrow.

"A puzzle before my first cup of coffee? How cruel."

Carlos's mouth quirked up at the corners as he zipped his jeans. "Oh, I think you can handle it."

Leine smiled and returned to the task. She turned the brick upside down and sideways and shook it with no results. She studied the surface, and noticed mortar still attached to one end. She pulled the mortar free, revealing a small slit. Leine shook the brick and a key fell into her hand.

"Clever," she said, replacing the key. "But why the change of heart? You didn't seem particularly interested in telling me last night."

He shrugged. His gaze met hers for an instant before he reached for his flight bag. Something inside Leine shifted, telling her to pay attention.

"Don't go." Her words tumbled out before she could stop herself. Eric's admonishment two days before echoed in her head.

He can take care of himself, Leine. Besides, you know the risks.

Carlos crossed the distance between them and drew her into his arms. She leaned her forehead on his chest. He smelled of soap and shampoo and the scent of a familiar lover. Leine tipped her chin up and kissed him. He returned in kind, his mouth both insistent and tender. Stepping back, he broke contact first.

"Time to go."

Leine nodded and took his offered arm, walking with him to the door. He cupped her face in his hands and kissed her softly.

"It's almost unbearable," he murmured.

"What?" Leine whispered.

"How much I love you."

Leine moved deeper into his embrace.

"Take care of yourself out there."

He smiled and ran his thumb along her cheek. Then he was gone.

Leine stared at the empty hallway for a few moments before she closed the door and moved into the kitchen. Saying goodbye before a job was always difficult. So many things could go wrong. Comforted with the knowledge he'd text her when he arrived at his destination, she poured herself a cup of coffee and added cream before grabbing her laptop to read the news. Half an hour later, she was having breakfast with April when her cell phone rang. It was Eric.

"Are you having a good weekend with our daughter?" he asked.

"What do you need?" Leine asked, trying but failing to mask her impatience.

"That's what I like about you, Leine. Brief and to the point. Rather like your working style, eh?"

"I'm eating breakfast with my daughter," she said, "so could you cut to the chase?"

His low chuckle grated on her nerves. "I've got the information on your next package. You'll be going to Campeche tomorrow morning. Pick up the packet at the usual place. This one's time sensitive. You'll only have a narrow window of opportunity to achieve the objective; a matter of hours, actually."

"So lovely there this time of year. I assume Lou will be assisting?"

"Not this time. I've got him occupied elsewhere. You'll be flying blind, I'm afraid."

"No problem." Eric was asking her to go old school. Although it was relatively odd to not have some form of remote support, it wasn't unheard of. Leine didn't mind working alone. But Lou was usually her point man on weapons and surveillance, which made things easier. Plus, she really liked him—he had a wicked sense of humor for a guy his age. Leine and Carlos took it upon themselves to give him a hard time about his impending retirement whenever they had the opportunity, which he took in good-natured stride.

"Mindy will set you up with accommodations. I'll give you Lou's contact there for whatever tools you need."

"Great." Leine glanced at April, who was trying hard not to look as though she were listening. She was failing miserably. "Anything else?" She wanted to spend whatever time she had left in San Francisco doing something fun with April, not wasting time talking on the phone with Eric.

"You'll be doing a back-to-back. I've received information that the other package we discussed earlier will be delivered two days from now." He paused. "Is that going to be a problem? If it is, let me know and I'll put Drysdale on it."

"That tool? Are you kidding me?" Leine shook her head. Curt Drysdale wasn't known for his elegant technique. The target would see him coming a mile away, which often made for a messy, spectacular kill of more than just the target. Some jobs required sensation. "Unless you're looking for ugly."

"That's what I thought. Check in with Mindy as soon as you take care of the first one. She'll have all the details. And Leine?"

"Yes?"

"Get some rest. You look like you haven't slept."

Leine stiffened as the line went dead. She turned and scanned the street below. He wasn't there. She lifted her gaze to the building across from the apartment. Empty windows stared back at her. *Did he install cameras in the apartment?* She scanned the living room. Doubtful. Carlos regularly swept his place for surveillance. Anger burned in her chest at the intrusion into her and Carlos's private lives. She grabbed a handful of curtain and yanked it across.

Too little, too late.

Why the hell did he feel the need to surveil her? A bad kind of shiver traced down her spine. She wasn't sneaking around. They hadn't been a couple in over ten years. Carlos's claims of their boss going off the reservation were sounding more and more likely. If he was right and Eric knew Carlos was collecting evidence against him, then things had just gotten much more dangerous for them both.

CHAPTER 7

Campeche, Mexico

LEINE EXITED THE plane at the airport in Campeche early the next evening. The asphalt radiated heat from the tropical sun into the claustrophobic night. The west side of the Yucatán Peninsula received several inches of rain throughout the summer, continuing well into fall. Not yet the dry winter season, the humidity was off the charts. As soon as she left the terminal her blouse adhered to her like she'd gone swimming fully clothed. She shrugged and picked away the material in the hopes of generating some kind of breeze.

She drove her rental car to her hotel, air conditioning blasting through the dashboard vents, stopping long enough at a market for some bug spray, a burner phone, and a bottle of good tequila.

Mindy had sent her to La Luna, a nondescript, out-of-the-way place run by an old friend of Mindy's—an ex-pat named Jasmine from Santa Clara. Steps from the beach, the guest rooms consisted of seven private studios built in a U-shape around an outdoor courtyard, used by guests to cook meals and hang out in the half-dozen hammocks strung between palms. She wouldn't be there long enough to meet any of the guests, though. Too bad. The warm ocean breeze and laid-back vibe would have done her a world of good. Maybe she'd bring Carlos and April there on a family vacation.

She dropped her things off at her room and made her way along a sandy path toward a nearby cantina. A gentle breeze riffled through her hair, which for a moment relieved the humidity. She smiled, happy the job wasn't somewhere frigid. Seawater lapped against her ankles as she plugged in the number for Lou's contact.

A few minutes later she ended the call, having memorized the address the guy gave her for a dead drop—a warehouse where she would retrieve the equipment she requested. When she arrived at the open-air cantina she chose a table near the water and ordered the special. Leine picked at her grilled fish and reread the dossier Eric had provided.

The target's name was Enrique Medina. A sicario, or hit man, for a well-known Mexican drug cartel, Medina had taken up moonlighting for a large energy consortium with ties to a rival political party unhappy with the recent presidential election.

In another life, Medina had been an underwater demolitions expert and had now been hired by the consortium to eliminate president-elect Felipe Calderón, slated to have dinner that evening on the largest oil platform in the Bay of Campeche. Not known for precision work, it was assumed Medina would blow the yacht used to ferry Calderón to and from the dinner. Heavily invested in a Calderón presidency, the US administration preferred the president-elect remain alive. Leine's orders were to stop Medina before he succeeded.

The dossier described in great detail the make and model of the boat and equipment Medina would be using, down to the insignia on his wetsuit. Leine assumed Eric had a contact within the consortium to have access to such precise information. The boat itself had a tracking device installed—Leine would monitor Medina's position from her laptop. A hardened veteran of the Mexican Marines, Medina was not a target to be taken lightly. There was only a narrow window of time in which to complete the mission, and she would have to do so in the dark and underwater.

She finished her dinner, paid the bill, and walked back to her casita to gather her things. She drove to the address given to her by her contact and cut the lights. The warehouse was one of several in a less desirable section of town. Shadows slanted across loading bays where functioning lights should have been. Leine scanned the buildings, looking for company.

Satisfied no one lurked nearby, she exited the vehicle and entered the warehouse by the side door as instructed. The light switch worked on the first try, illuminating a filthy interior buttressed only by chipped paint and damp, deteriorating concrete. A rat scurried along the far wall, searching for escape.

A metal table stood to Leine's right. On top rested two boxes. One held rebreather diving gear, a pair of fins, and night-vision goggles. The other contained a modified speargun, a wicked-looking diver's knife, and a digital underwater camera. Alongside the table was a one-man DPV, or Diver Propulsion Vehicle. Made of aluminum, the DPV was lightweight and could be used with a rebreather, and would get her to the target much more quickly than if she were to swim under her own power.

After checking the gear, Leine loaded the equipment into the trunk of the car and drove to the waterfront, where she booted up her laptop and initiated the tracking program. Immediately, a red dot appeared on the screen, identifying Medina's powerboat. It was currently off shore six kilometers to the northeast and moving fast. Leine continued on to a small marina where she transferred the equipment to a nondescript powerboat. Only one other vessel appeared occupied, but it was on the far side of the marina. Other than that, the place was deserted.

She did a walk-through to make sure everything was in working order and that the additional fuel she'd requested was onboard. With no one to see her, Leine slipped away from the dock and quietly motored through the darkness, following the blinking red light.

Half a kilometer from where the red dot had ceased moving, she cut the engine and dropped anchor. Positioning herself at the bow, she sighted on Medina's boat with the NVGs, searching for movement. A man in full dive gear perched on the swim platform near the stern. Tall and well muscled, Medina—if it was him— would be difficult to subdue if it came to close-range combat. She double-checked the speargun. There was enough charge to shoot from a good distance, but taking into account the distortion and drag of shooting underwater she didn't want to be more than a meter from her target. That meant she'd have to be ready to execute upon approach—ideally while moving.

The man climbed aboard what looked like a large DPV floating next to the boat. The size of the vehicle meant it was capable of carrying a payload in addition to a diver, which meant he was heading to the yacht with the explosives. The man released the lines holding the DPV fast and disappeared below the surface.

Several minutes later and with the rebreather gear on, Leine attached the speargun to her DPV, submerged, and headed toward her target. The adrenaline hadn't yet kicked in but would soon enough. The water temperature was comfortable and visibility good. Leine relaxed into the ride, guiding the DPV with her fins as the submersible cut through the alternating currents like a machete through whipped cream. The eerie green glow from the night vision goggles helped her avoid anything solid that might interrupt her journey.

As she approached the target's boat, Leine dialed back the propulsion and coasted silently toward the vessel. This was the tricky part. If for some reason Medina had returned, she'd show up on sonar like a big damn fish. Maybe he'd take notice, maybe he wouldn't. It depended upon whether he kept the sound turned up on his equipment.

Unlikely.

Leine parked the DPV on the sea floor, took note of its location, and swam to the boat. She shadowed the hull, scanning underneath in case Medina returned, drifting upward until her head emerged just enough to clear the surface. She detected no movement on the boat itself. She re-submerged and glided to the stern, then slowly surfaced. She waited, listening, knowing that as soon as she attempted to board, if Medina was back on the boat she'd have to be quick. She unsheathed the diver's knife strapped to her thigh and put it between her teeth.

Slowly, she raised herself onto the diving platform, making sure her body weight was equally distributed so the boat wouldn't list to one side. Leine took a few deep breaths to calm herself, glad for the sharp awareness that accompanied an adrenaline surge.

Not hearing anything, Leine rose to a crouch and peered over the railing. A faint glow shone through the cracks in the cabin door. Curtains covered the windows, blocking the rest of the light from inside.

The lack of movement suggested that Medina wasn't onboard, but she remained cautious. Someone else might be resting below decks. Leine crept to the door, taking note of anything lying nearby that could be used as a weapon. There wasn't much. Looked like Medina kept a clean boat.

Leine eased the door open and scanned the empty cabin. Other than the keys dangling from the ignition, nothing had been left lying out. She rummaged through the console until she found the boat's registration. Medina wasn't listed as the owner of record. She replaced the documents and moved forward. It was possible Medina didn't bring identification, although taking the chance of being boarded by the Mexican Navy without papers would have a deleterious effect on carrying out his bosses' wishes.

Not finding anything in the main cabin, Leine pulled out a small flashlight and continued searching—she first checked the head, followed by the two forward cabins.

Medina's passport was in the second cabin, hidden under the mattress. The picture was typical of passport photos and showed a dark-haired man sporting a full beard and mustache, his eyes obscured by a pair of thick, black-rimmed glasses. Facial hair seemed an odd choice for a diver, although he could have shaved prior to the job.

Satisfied she'd accurately identified her target, Leine replaced the document and did a cursory once-over of the small closet. There she discovered a nine millimeter and an MP5 submachine gun with sufficient rounds to fend off a small army.

Strange, Leine mused. AK-47s were usually the weapon of choice for cartel thugs. Easy to get, and, for the most part, worry-free. But, the guy *was* a hit man for a drug cartel. Depending on which cartel, the money was there for whatever weapons he wanted.

Leine sheathed her knife and walked back to the dive platform. She paused, getting her bearings. Less than a kilometer away, the oil rig's lights glowed in the darkness. It wouldn't take long to reach using the DPV. Leine slipped into the water and swam back to the scooter.

Using the night vision goggles, she sped toward the platform, searching the terrain ahead in case Medina aborted the mission and was on his way back. Water rushed past, pushing at her facemask, and she secured her grip on the harpoon.

One of the legs of the oil platform materialized several meters in front of her and she slowed, scanning for Medina. She caught a glimpse of the back of his wetsuit and fins below the surface near the president-elect's yacht. Leine pushed forward slowly, mindful of creating a disturbance and alerting her quarry. She circled behind him, slowly curving upward, narrowing the gap. Intent on his work, he didn't notice her approach from below. When she was at the optimal distance, Leine aimed the speargun and pulled the trigger.

The barb hit him center mass. She'd been aiming for his heart. Medina writhed and twisted, frantically trying to dislodge the harpoon. Dark green through the NVGs, a stream of blood leaked from the wound. A package, most likely explosives, sank toward the bottom. Leine throttled forward and at the same time unsheathed the knife.

Unable to get a clear shot at his throat, she slid by him and sliced through his air hose.

Too close. Medina's fist connected with the side of Leine's head, knocking her goggles aside and filling her mask with water. Blindly, she jammed the throttle forward and sped out of reach.

She cleared the mask and reset the goggles in time to see Medina float toward the surface. She threw the DPV into gear and raced after him to finish the job.

She didn't need to. He was dead. Mask still on with his mouth open and his arms and legs extended, he floated gracefully in the gentle current, the spear still lodged in his chest.

Mindful of the sharks that patrolled the bay, Leine brought out the underwater camera and snapped several photographs of the body—Eric's contact had requested proof. Normally, she would weigh down the target so that the body wouldn't be found, but the contact had wanted Medina used as a warning.

Finished, she stowed the camera and checked the hull for explosives. Medina had managed to set two along the stern, but he hadn't attached a detonator. Rather than possibly alerting the yacht's occupants by removing Medina's work, Leine left the plastique in place. There would be no explosion tonight.

Satisfied that she'd completed her mission, she checked the compass on her watch to get her bearings before she returned to the DPV and headed back to her boat.

CHAPTER 8

LEINE WOKE THE next morning with last night's libations still riding her tongue. Perspiration streamed down her face from the grisly image of Medina's floating corpse—the latest specter in a never-ending loop of nightmares featuring the targets she'd killed. She reached for a tissue on the nightstand and knocked over the bottle of tequila.

It was empty.

She shook her head to clear it and put her hand on the mattress to steady herself as the room took a hard spin to the left. Hot bile crept into her throat with nausea close behind. Where the hell was she again?

Oh. Right. Campeche. Time to call Mindy.

Head down, she crawled from the bed and staggered to the bathroom, the tequila's aftertaste adding to her already significant nausea. Sleep was getting harder to come by, and the agave elixir could be counted on to put her down for the count.

She wasn't fond of the repercussions.

Steadying herself with her hands on the rim of the sink, she stared into the mirror at the dark circles beneath her bloodshot eyes. The job was finally getting to her.

Before, she'd skate past inconvenient feelings and memories, stuffing everything into neat little compartments in her brain, rarely letting anything out for inspection. But now, the frequency of the nightmares and the ghosts of jobs past had her wondering how much longer she could continue doing what she did, much less stay alive.

She drifted into the present and frowned at herself. Her hair had escaped the confines of its usual ponytail and bobby pins and stuck out at odd angles. A wry smile tugged at her lips when she thought of what Carlos would say if he saw her.

The idea of being able to talk to Carlos about the job she'd done the night before helped ground her, and she shook off the self-doubt. She turned on the faucet and leaned over to gulp the cool water. One of the lucky few who could eat and drink anything, anywhere, Leine rarely suffered tourista's revenge. Besides, whatever remained of the tequila in her stomach would most likely take care of any nasty parasites even thinking of hitching a ride.

After a scalding hot shower and several cups of strong coffee from La Luna's proprietress, Leine called Eric's assistant, Mindy, to find out where she was going next.

"Amsterdam. There's a ticket waiting for you at Campeche International. And Leine?" Mindy's voice had apology written all over it.

"Let me guess. Long layover?"

"Sorry. The only flights available were through Mexico City with some pretty hefty wait times. Otherwise, you have your choice of milk runs—two, three stops. Eric insisted I get you in country within twenty-four hours."

"Is he at least putting me up somewhere decent?"

"Absolutely. Amsterdam Gardens. A room near the back. There's Wi-Fi and a restful little courtyard where you can unwind."

"Thanks, Mindy."

Leine ended the call and dug through her things for the camera she'd used to verify Medina's body. She removed the memory card and pushed it into the slot on her laptop and then connected her agency-issued cell phone. Once the laptop registered the connection, she encrypted and uploaded a file containing the photos and a prearranged code to Eric's private message board on the deep web. Afterward, she wiped the images off the card and stashed the camera in her carry-on bag.

Leine traveled light and was packed in minutes. With one last scan of the room to make sure she hadn't left anything, she drove to the warehouse to return the equipment, and then headed for the airport.

She napped maybe an hour on the plane to Mexico City. Once she landed, she treated herself to a decent meal while she downloaded and skimmed the dossier on her next target, Emile Robicheaux.

Born in Martinique, Robicheaux first appeared on the arms scene in 2002. A wunderkind financial whiz in Paris in the late nineties, he determined early on that dealing in black market weapons and ammunition yielded a much better return on investment than stocks or real estate ever would. The first mention of his penchant for killing off the competition surfaced in 2005, when he and two other gunmen stormed a black market small arms convention being held in Warsaw. It was there that he'd cemented his reputation as a coldblooded killer intent on eliminating the competition by allowing only one witness to survive any deal he did not sanction. Robicheaux's typed manifesto declared his intentions to control the industry and he was close to achieving his goal. As of that day, he was considered second only to Adrian "The Wolf" Volkov—the largest illicit arms dealer in the world.

Leine managed a few more hours of fitful sleep on the flight to Amsterdam, but the large man sleeping next to her in business class sounded like a bulldozer and earplugs didn't help. She ordered a glass of wine, but sleep continued to elude her. Leine stared out the window at the clouds below and wondered how her daughter was doing, imagining a time when she and Carlos would retire and actually be a family.

Nice dream.

Thoughts of the last time Carlos had stayed with her and April at their home in the vineyard surfaced, and she smiled at the memory. It was during harvest that fall. Carlos and April were deep in conversation about the differences between wines and sugar content, or brix, when Leine overheard them talking outside on the porch.

"Do you notice the difference in aroma?" Carlos had asked. "When you smell the cabernet, what does it remind you of?"

April took a deep whiff of the glass Carlos had poured. "It's kind of fruity—like blackberries?"

Carlos nodded. "Good. Anything else?"

"Chocolate? But there's something more."

Carlos waited, watching her think.

"It reminds me of the cedar chest in my room."

"Exactly. Good job." Carlos smiled and poured another glass, this time from a bottle of merlot.

"How about this one?" he said, sliding it toward her.

April wrinkled her nose. "It smells more like the earth." At Carlos's prompting, she sniffed again. "Plums. Definitely plums, but really smoky."

"That's merlot. The smokiness is from the oak barrels it's aged in. You're pretty good at this, you know that?" Carlos opened the last bottle, deftly handling the two-pronged cork puller. "Okay. Last one." He poured a couple of ounces of burgundy-colored wine into a third glass and slid it across the table. They'd have to invite their neighbors over to help finish the bottles, Leine mused.

April leaned over and inhaled deeply, then sat back and cocked her head to the side.

"A cross between black cherries and pepper."

Carlos grinned. "Yup. Zinfandel is known for its peppery taste."

"I thought Zinfandel was pink?"

"That's White Zinfandel—they remove the skins while it's in the tank to give it that characteristic rosé color. Zin's actually a red grape, originally brought over from Italy a long time ago. And," he added, glancing at Leine, standing in the doorway, "it's your mom's favorite wine. At the moment."

The plane hit a pocket of turbulence, jolting Leine back to the present. She sighed and took another sip of wine. Not as good as the stuff made from her landlord's grapes. Maybe, when she got back home, she'd see if he'd be willing to sell the place. She liked the idea of retiring and settling down in Napa Valley with their own vineyard.

At least she had good memories of Amsterdam. Arriving at Schiphol almost felt like home.

Almost.

Leine headed straight for Schiphol Plaza and a train to the city center. The abrupt change from the tropical climate of Campeche to the cool fall weather in the Netherlands had her digging through her carry-on for a jacket. She stopped at a kiosk to exchange several hundred dollars for euros. Half an hour later she found her hotel, and checked in as Eve Mason.

She dropped her bags on the bed and checked the time. 16:10. Just after seven in the morning on the West

Coast. Eric would be awake. She logged in to a secure site run by the Agency and clicked to make a video call.

Eric's tanned face materialized. By the looks of him, he was well rested and still in his kitchen, having coffee.

"Good morning," he said, stifling a yawn. "Or should I say good afternoon?"

"Checking in. I'm in Amsterdam." Leine was too tired to keep a leash on her impatience. She needed to get on with this and then get back to April and Carlos. And sleep for a week.

"Good afternoon, Eric. It's good to see you. How are you?" Eric said in a feminine voice, mocking her clipped tone.

Ignoring him, Leine glanced at the notes she'd made on Robicheaux. "I have an address, some cryptic information, and a shitty photograph, but nowhere in the file does it say when the package will be available. I assume contact is imminent?" Otherwise, why the hell did he need her there so quickly?

Eric nodded and tilted his head to one side, stretching his neck. "You're right about that. You're to go to Café Ryker on Lauriergracht Canal, at precisely twenty-one hundred. Our friend is scheduled to meet a Russian agent posing as an arms dealer. Word is he's in the market for aircraft."

"Then why do you need me there? Can't the Russians take him out?"

"Our Russian counterpart prefers to remain undercover. The Frenchman isn't the only quarry they're after. If things go south too many other operations would be at risk." Eric shrugged. "Besides, if he does have moles inside Russian intelligence, then he might be able to identify whoever they used." His gaze dropped to the cup in his hand. He took another sip of coffee. "And, as I explained before, they want the best."

Acid burned in her gut. *Be careful with this one, Leine. Something isn't right.*

"Who gave you the intel?" Leine leaned back in her chair, working to keep her voice modulated. "Can you trust them?"

"I realize you're gun-shy because of the Glushenko incident, but trust me, I've vetted this source for months. He's clean."

"Of course. Do I have any support on this one?"

"Lou's still on another job, but I can assign someone if you feel you need them." Eric took another sip of coffee and set it back down. "You seem to have managed on your own in Mexico. The PRI is indebted to you, as is the United States government."

Leine rolled her eyes. She hated it when he cloaked himself and the Agency in the flag. She was perfectly aware she and the other operatives worked in that murky area considered off-book. No matter what happened when securing the nation's interests, the decision makers didn't want to know anything except that the job was done.

"What about Carlos?" Leine asked. "We work well together and know each other's style." Most jobs didn't last more than a few days, so he would have checked in, unless he was collecting intel for further operations.

Some kind of emotion flickered across Eric's face too quickly for Leine to identify. Irritation? Anger? Carlos might have been right about Eric's jealousy, she thought.

"I haven't heard from Carlos. He was supposed to call in last night."

She sat forward. "That doesn't sound like him." Memories of Carlos's demeanor the day he left the apartment came rushing back. *Relax, Leine. He's fine. Don't jump to conclusions.*

"No, it doesn't. That's why I've decided to give him more time before we dissociate."

Leine's fingers itched to grab her boss around his perfectly tanned throat. "What do you mean, 'dissociate'? You're joking, right? He's been with the Agency for ten years. *Ten years.* Doesn't that mean anything to you?" Her cheeks heated as anger spiked in her chest. "You should send all available personnel to his last location to search for him."

She rose from her chair and strode to the window. Leaves from a nearby tree littered the private patio, staining the bricks red.

"Calm down, Leine. I have every faith in him. He's only a day late. I'm sure he lost his phone, or something as equally simple as that."

Leine walked back to the laptop and glared at Eric. "Send someone now, Eric. You can't afford to lose him."

Eric's eyes glittered at the warning in her voice. "No, I can't." He stared back, matching her expression.

"Tell me where he is," she said, crossing her arms. "If I'm close, I can catch a flight once I'm finished with Robicheaux."

"You're not. Like I said, I'll give him one more day and then we'll send in a recovery team. Is that okay with you?" His voice dripped sarcasm.

It wasn't, but there was little Leine could do if he wouldn't tell her where Carlos was. She could always try Mindy, although that might be a hard sell. She was loyal to Eric.

"So we're good?" Eric asked, his expression stern as he went into business mode. "You have everything you need?"

"No, we're not good. But as long as you gave Spartacus a heads-up that I'd be in town, then yes, I'm fine."

Eric nodded. "Spartacus is expecting you, and he'll have what you need. Good luck, Leine. I'll wait for your call."

The screen went black, and Leine closed her laptop. Tendrils of worry etched their way into her mind.

Where was Carlos? Eric was within his rights not telling her his location. He probably feared she'd put her current mission on hold in order to go to his side.

He'd be right.

As far as she was concerned, the job with the Frenchman could wait.

CHAPTER 9

LEINE FRESHENED UP and walked to a nearby Indian restaurant for dinner. Then she hopped on a tram and headed for a bookshop in Old Town where Spartacus was located. She'd used him and his extensive contacts for several jobs in the past and she trusted him. Well, as far as she could trust a man who had no past and who supplied anything to anyone, no questions asked. So far, he'd never let her down.

Situated in a centuries-old building originally built for a member of the banking community, Spartacus's shop took up minimal space on the ground floor near the back. Hidden as it was in an unassuming corner of the building, the only way anyone would be able to find it was through word of mouth. Often, even that wasn't enough. It was a good thing his main business wasn't books.

The door opened to the sound of a tiny bell jingling above her head. Leine stifled a sneeze as she entered. Sunlight streamed through a narrow window, illuminating a blizzard of dust particles sent spinning in frenzied abandon as she walked past. The dark wood beams and high white ceiling did little to dispel the claustrophobe's nightmare; the seemingly endless shelves of books stacked floor-to-ceiling and way too much furniture gave the room the ambiance of a hoarder's dream. She picked her way carefully through stacks of newspapers and magazines and around chairs piled high with magazines and more books, marveling at how each was able to maintain verticality.

Phlegmy wheezing preceded the owner by several beats. As she waited for Spartacus to appear, Leine glanced at several of the titles in the bookcases. Most were in Dutch—a language she spoke with only rudimentary skill.

"Well, well. I've been expecting you." The smile on Spartacus's face put her at ease and she smiled in return. The buttons on his wrinkled blue shirt barely contained his soft beer belly, although the brown, moth-eaten sweater he wore over the top of ancient chinos worked hard in his favor.

"It's good to see you, Sparky." Leine leaned in and they kissed each other's cheeks. "It's been a while."

Spartacus, or Sparky for short, waved a doughy hand in the air, dismissing her comments. "With friends like you, the length of time matters little. It always feels as though we parted last week." He placed the book he'd been carrying on a nearby stack of papers and crooked his finger, indicating she follow him. He pressed a button concealed in an old brass lamp, and a section of bookcase swung open to reveal a hidden room. They stepped through, and he closed the door behind them.

"Eric made it clear that I was to do everything I could to accommodate your requests." He shuffled around a long, scarred counter in the middle of the room. Passport blanks from different countries lay stacked on one end, with a half dozen in various stages of completion taking up residence in the center. A paper cutter and row of official-looking stamps graced the other end.

"You've been busy," Leine observed. A few of the pictures were duplicates, some weren't.

"Yes, several clients requested passports in anticipation of the RFID requirement." RFID stood for radio frequency identification, and the US government was now requiring all new passports to have the chip. Most European countries had already adopted the technology.

"Will it affect business?"

He shrugged. "Not much. It isn't hard to duplicate the chip. In a few years it will be even easier." He grinned, his rosy cheeks pushing deep creases to the outer corner of his eyes. "Thank heavens. Passports are my bread and butter."

US passports were valid for ten years. Within that time, the older ones containing the original computer chips would be vulnerable to new technology: scanners, encryption, whatever the criminal mind could dream up to circumvent government's attempts to keep the information safe and forgers stymied. Sparky's business model would be viable for years to come.

They chatted a bit about how fast technology was changing and moved on to Sparky's grandchildren before Leine steered the conversation back to her original reason for being there.

"In addition to the equipment Eric requested, I need a tactical knife with a six-inch blade and a VSS sniper rifle with a night scope, suppressor, bipod, and ammunition. I'd also like a US passport."

Sparky gave her a sharp glance. "Eric did not mention the additional requests. I will have to recalculate the charges."

"Bill me for the extras. I'd appreciate if you wouldn't mention this."

Sparky nodded. One of the things she liked most about him: no questions.

"It will take some time." He waved at the unfinished forgeries on the table in front of him. "There are several ahead of you."

Leine pulled a wad of euros from her pocket. "Here's a down payment. I'm happy to pay for expedited processing. On all of it."

Sparky smiled and took the money. "We understand each other, don't we?"

Leine nodded. "Yes, I think we do."

Two hours later, Leine had everything she requested except the passport. Sparky had the weapons she needed stored in a secret room hidden behind a false wall in a closet. He'd secured the rifle and scope in anticipation of Leine's visit, as it was her preferred weapon. He'd found it odd that Eric hadn't ordered one beforehand.

The extra money Leine had given the supplier pushed all but one of the clients clamoring for new passports to the back of the line. Sparky had explained that the passport ahead of hers couldn't be delayed. The client was only in town for a short time and had paid handsomely—more so than Leine—for the expedited work. Hers would be ready by morning, which in retrospect would be fine. Her lack of sleep was beginning to show, albeit in small ways. The tremor in her left hand worried her most. She could do with a rest before heading back to the States.

With a few hours to spare, Leine decided to walk to the café and check out the neighborhood before finding the best vantage point. Normally, she'd have a few days to become familiar with the target's habits: when and what they ate, whether they were night owls or not, who they spent time with. Not that rush jobs were unusual, but after the Glushenko incident Leine was wary. Shouldering a backpack she'd picked up earlier that day containing the weapons and other tools she needed for the job, she set off toward Lauriergracht Canal.

There was a bite to the crisp fall air signifying winter's approach, and Leine pulled her jacket tighter to ward off the chill. She loved walking through Amsterdam. The low-key city had a relaxed, experienced feel, like a woman of a certain age making her way home in the early morning hours, trailing the scent of sex and too much wine behind her. Leine enjoyed the Dutch and their pragmatic approach to life, and looked forward to her visits even though most of the time she was only passing through. It was a rare occasion that she was tasked with actually completing a job here. Usually the city was a jumping-off point to the rest of Europe—a place to secure what she'd need before heading to other locales.

The neighborhood where the café was located held a mixture of old and new. Lauriergracht Canal boasted several cars and bicycles parked along its banks, its dark waters mirroring the streetlights now blinking on as dusk descended. The Ryker Café occupied the lower floor of an imposing brick building dating from the seventeenth century. Originally a wealthy merchant's home, the curved gables and red roof lent its façade the iconic presence of the Dutch Golden Age. It stood shoulder to shoulder with similar structures, interspersed with modern, gleaming storefronts advertising the latest in tech and fashion.

Leine stepped to the side as a bicycle whooshed past, piloted by a young man wrapped in a patterned neck scarf. Taking her time, she walked toward the café, unobtrusively scanning the exterior, making note of the buildings and streets nearby.

Once inside, she walked to the counter and ordered a cup of tea. Small clusters of patrons sat at round tables and in secluded booths, speaking in hushed tones. A popular spot, apparently. Not what she was expecting. Eric had recommended she set up inside the café, which made his requisition for a handgun understandable, but the idea didn't sit well with her now that she was there.

Leine moved to a small table near the back, memorizing the layout as she did. The space was dark and crowded—not conducive to an easy kill or escape. Allowing the Frenchman to enter the space would complicate matters and put innocent bystanders at risk. It would also expose her to potential witnesses.

No, she'd have to finish the job before he walked in the door. The server brought her tea, and she sipped it while considering her options. Close-quarters assassination would make verification of the target easy— the only thing that would be easy. Everything depended on how heavily guarded Robicheaux was. The advantage of using the rifle from across the street was twofold: she'd be gone before anyone knew what happened, and she could control casualties.

Leine finished her tea, paid the proprietor, and walked back outside to catalog the neighborhood's tactical locations, ingress, egress, and choke points. Turning right onto a bridge, she crossed over the canal and walked along the other side, turning onto a quiet side street. She stopped and waited near a building with a low roofline situated between two taller structures with darkened windows. The window ledges combined with the iron wall anchors created a zigzag route to the roof and would be an easy climb—the only difficulty would be to accomplish it unnoticed. She scanned the immediate area for passersby and waited as several bicyclists approached, hunched against the chill. After they rode past, Leine tightened the straps on the backpack and stepped closer to the building. She checked her surroundings once more before she grabbed hold of the lowest windowsill and pulled herself up.

She'd made it to the third set of windows before a pedestrian appeared and she stilled, waiting for them to pass. Once they'd gone, she continued until she reached the roofline, and climbed over the top. She moved to the canal side of the building and set the bag down, and checked her watch. Forty-five minutes until Robicheaux was scheduled to meet the Russian agent. Leine removed the rifle components from the bag and put them together, and set up the bipod. Then she flipped open the scope covers to sight the café across the canal.

Perfect.

CHAPTER 10

LEINE CLOSED HER eyes to absorb her surroundings. The distant sound of traffic and briny scent of canal water in the cool air transported her back in time to a trip she'd taken to Amsterdam with Carlos several years before. They'd shared a romantic dinner and one too many bottles of wine before winding their way back to their cozy hotel room. Carlos had been a fount of information on the architecture and history of the area, spouting little-known facts, and made the neighborhood come alive in a way she hadn't experienced before. She'd developed a deep appreciation for the people who settled Amsterdam and would never look at the city the same way again.

A boat with happy partiers cruised by on the canal, breaking through her reverie, and she focused on the café. The reassuring weight of the handgun against her back and the knife strapped to her calf gave the illusion of preparedness.

Who was she kidding? Not enough sleep, not enough time, not enough information. Eric rarely gave her jobs this sketchy and hadn't ever scheduled a back-to-back. She *could* cut bait and return to her room for some much-needed sleep. But she'd just have to try again, and the location might not be as good the next time. Plus, there'd be the added headache of having to deal with Eric's anger. She glanced at the rifle and mentally shrugged off her reservations. The repercussions weren't worth it.

Might as well finish the job since I'm here.

Leine took a moment to center herself before settling in with the rifle. Drumming her fingers on the roof, she wondered why Carlos hadn't checked in yet. It wasn't like him, and she was worried. She dug in the backpack for the burner phone that had been in the equipment Spartacus gave her and glanced at the screen. No messages. Her concern growing, she fired off a text asking him to message her, and returned the phone to her bag.

The young man wearing the patterned scarf Leine had noticed earlier pedaled to the front of the café and climbed off his bike. He parked near the entrance and shrugged off his backpack before going inside. Twenty minutes later, he reappeared, straddled the bike, and set off down the street.

The gods are with you tonight, she thought. He'd be long gone by the time Robicheaux arrived. Not that she anticipated a gunfight—if all went as planned, the Frenchman would be the only casualty—but a lack of innocent bystanders was ideal.

A few minutes before 21:00 a black sedan pulled up to the café and two men got out. One was huge and wore dark glasses that didn't cover the ugly scars along his face; the other was shorter and had a hat pulled low on his forehead, obscuring his features.

Leine peered through the scope, trying to make out if the one in the hat might be Robicheaux, but she couldn't be certain. More than likely they were advance security and the Frenchman was still inside the car, or would show later in another vehicle.

The two men scanned the area surrounding the café. Apparently satisfied, the man in the hat opened the back door of the sedan and stepped aside. Drawing a bead just above the open door, Leine took the slack out of the trigger and waited. Just then, a van bearing the logo of a local beer distributor pulled up, blocking her view.

Damn. There was now only a partial view of the sedan's trunk. She waited a few beats, willing the vehicle to move, but the driver's side door opened and a man holding a clipboard got out.

Leine scanned the street below her. There weren't any cars or pedestrian traffic nearby. Leaving the rifle, she grabbed her pack and scrambled over the roof's edge. The climb down took much less time than reaching the roof, and she sprinted across the boulevard toward the bridge, sliding the semiauto from her waistband as she did. Staying low, she moved quickly along the canal, keeping the van and the trunk of the sedan in her sights. As she stepped onto the bridge, movement caught her eye. Partially obscured by a tree, the young man in the scarf stood in the shadows next to his bike at the end of the bridge, his attention riveted on the café. Leine stopped short. There was something different.

The backpack.

The material sagged across his back, drooping like a deflated tire. Earlier, when he'd gone into the café, the pack had been full.

Leine shoved her gun into her waistband and sprinted across the bridge toward him. As she drew near, the cell phone in his hand came into view. Still focused on the café, he didn't hear her approach until seconds before she reached him.

She was too late.

The explosion ripped through the night, throwing them both to the ground. Glass splintered, showering the sidewalk, and pieces of brick and burning debris arced through the air, landing in the street yards away.

Ears ringing, Leine rolled to her feet. For a moment, all motion ceased, as though the world was catching its breath.

Then the screaming began.

The cries of survivors pierced the still night. The young man, no more than a teenager, scrambled to his feet and turned to run. Leine tackled him and shoved him to the ground. He landed face first and hard. The air left his lungs with a loud *ooph*.

"You're not going anywhere." Leine wrestled his arms behind him and knelt on his back to keep him still as she surveyed the damage.

Glass shards lay on the street next to the van, its windows blown out from the blast. The sedan hadn't fared any better. Flames licked at the empty windows of the café, and black smoke streamed through a gaping hole on the side of the building. Bricks and glass littered the sidewalk. The driver of the van lay on his back in the middle of the street, a pool of blood surrounding his head.

A man appeared at the entrance, arm clutched around a sobbing woman, her shirt drenched in blood. They staggered outside, followed by three more, all of whom were coughing. Two were covered in blood. One man didn't appear to have suffered any damage, although the look on his face told Leine he was in a state of shock.

"What are you doing? Let me go," the kid cried, his voice muffled by his prone position.

A familiar accent.

"You're Russian?" she asked.

"Let me go," he repeated, his voice weak.

"Not likely," Leine said, her heart racing as she scanned the survivors for Robicheaux. The kid struggled against her. Leine pressed harder and he gave up, his body going limp. His cell phone was lying next to him on the ground, and she picked it up and slid it into her pocket. She patted him down, paying particular attention to his backpack, but he didn't have a weapon.

The big man with the scars who'd exited the sedan before the bomb went off staggered from the café. Blood streamed down the side of his head onto his shirt. No one else followed. Sirens wailed in the distance. Leine had to find out if the Frenchman had made it inside the café and if he was dead, and she needed to do it now, before the police arrived.

She lifted her knee from the kid's back and stood, yanking him to his feet before she wrenched his hands up between his shoulder blades. He didn't cry out.

"Who do you work for?" Leine pulled her gun, shoved it into his back, and propelled him toward the side street next to the café. "Who were you trying to kill?"

The kid kept his mouth shut. Leine put more pressure on his arm. He winced and a small cry escaped his lips.

"I don't have time to fuck around here. I will break your arm and probably worse if you don't tell me. Now."

His face impassive, he set his lips in a hard line. Leine wrenched his arm to the breaking point. Wincing, he stumbled. Tears of pain streaked from the corners of his eyes and rolled down his cheeks.

"I—a friend of my uncle's. I don't know his name."

"Who were you sent to kill?" They were close to the café, approaching from the side. No one paid any attention to them.

"A French murderer."

"Name."

His expression hardened. Leine pulled him up short and pressed the gun more firmly into his back. "If you don't tell me what you know, you won't be of use to me and I will give you up to the police. You'll be tried as a terrorist."

"Emile Robicheaux." He spat on the sidewalk.

"How do you know this Robicheaux was inside when you detonated the bomb?"

An emotion—fear? uncertainty?—shadowed his features and he looked at the ground. "I knew," he said with a defiant shrug.

"You knew jack shit. Do you have any idea how many innocent people were inside that café? You realize you likely killed more than the Frenchman, right? *If* you even got him." Leine's face heated, her anger spiking at the boy's idiotic, amateur attempt. There were far better ways of eliminating a target than remote-controlled explosives. Ones with much lower casualties.

"Sometimes many must suffer when the good of the whole is compromised."

Leine checked her urge to slap the self-righteous smirk off the boy's face. "Just stop with the martyrdom bullshit, all right?"

They reached the side of the café, and Leine shoved him up against the brick wall.

"Your uncle's friend, does he work for anyone? SVR? GRU?" Was this an example of one Russian organization not knowing what the other was doing? Possible, but not probable.

He stared at the ground, his expression unreadable. She wrenched his arm again and shoved him harder into the wall.

He groaned. "Yes. No. I don't know." The words were sandwiched between short, explosive breaths.

The sirens were getting louder. Leine yanked him away from the wall and frog-marched him next to the gaping hole in the café.

"What's your name?"

"Why, are you going to call my mother?"

Leine almost laughed at the sarcasm. "You know, that's not a bad idea. I have your phone. I'll bet she'd be interested in what you've done."

"Please don't call her." Panic laced his words. "My name is Ilya." He strained to look through the opening, but Leine pulled him back.

"Not so fast."

"But I have to know if the Frenchman is dead. Please, I must look."

"It's possible you may not recognize him."

"I would know the rat-fuck anywhere."

"Not if his head's blown off." She surveyed the damage to the seventeenth-century wall. "What were you trying to do, take the entire building down?"

His cheeks reddened. "I wanted to be certain…" His words trailed off.

She checked the street behind them. When she was sure no one was watching, she stepped over the bricks and through the hole, dragging Ilya behind her.

The café was unrecognizable. The explosives had ripped through the wooden bar, leaving a gaping hole in its wake, and sent tables and chairs like missiles into the booths and walls. Several bodies fanned out from the blast site, as though they'd been flung through the air by an angry giant. Ceiling tiles littered the floor, the light fixtures warped into grotesque sculptures.

Leine gagged at the smell of charred flesh and toxic, melted plastic, and took shallow breaths through her mouth. She pulled out a small flashlight and quickly walked Ilya by first one dead body and then another, but he was unable to identify any of them as Robicheaux. A few had burned beyond recognition but Leine discounted these as they didn't match the Frenchman's size or gender. Ilya's face blanched at the sight and smell of the charred flesh and looked away, retching as he did.

When they'd covered the sections of the building that were accessible, including the bathrooms, Leine and Ilya headed back toward the blast hole in the wall. By the sound of the sirens, first responders were only seconds away. Leine pushed Ilya out onto the street and followed him into the shadows.

Lights strobed against the building opposite the café as emergency personnel pulled up to the entrance. Leine hurried Ilya down a dark side street, away from the shouting and chaos, unsure of what to do with the young Russian.

Or how she was going to find the Frenchman.

Emile Robicheaux looked out the window at the black smoke billowing from the café as his car sped past. They'd been less than a block away when the bomb went off. He shifted in his seat, uncomfortable in the Kevlar vest. He wasn't about to take it off.

Funny, he thought they'd use a sniper. Or, at the very least, poison. Maybe even a knife concealed in an assassin's coat sleeve, or a garrote, although that would have been a last resort. He'd prepared for those methods. The bomb had been a surprise. Messy. Amateurish.

Not up to standards.

Fortunately, Oscar made it out alive. Robicheaux ordered his driver to pull over long enough to pluck his friend from the sidewalk. He'd sustained a deep gash on the side of his head, to which he held a handkerchief with limited success. Blood soaked the side of his face and down his coat, contributing to the giant man's fearsome appearance.

"I thought you said there wasn't a problem," Robicheaux said. Oscar had called to give the all clear—right before the bomb went off.

"As far as I could tell, everything was according to plan." Oscar shook his head. "The Russian is dead. His bodyguards didn't survive, either."

"So, the bomber could have been targeting either of us."

The demise of the potential aircraft supplier came at an unfortunate time. The Frenchman's business was exploding—he smiled inwardly at his play on words—and more planes were imperative if he were to expand. Now he'd have to find another supplier he could trust.

Not easy in his world.

The bomb worried him. His associate could have been marked for death by some terrorist faction, but the theory had holes. Robicheaux had checked the man's credentials and there'd been no evidence of dissatisfied customers. Nor was there anything in his background that would suggest ties to fanatics—other than having dealt with some of the nasty characters who frequented the shadowy black market of the arms world. And even those types wouldn't chew off the hand that fed them.

Indeed, the man had a stellar reputation, as far as criminals went.

That left the possibility that either the Russians used an incompetent assassin, which wasn't likely, or more than one group wanted him dead.

Much more likely.

He had to admit, he was disappointed they hadn't sent the *Léopard*. His face grew warm just thinking about what he'd do with her when he captured the mysterious assassin. The torture would be exquisite to watch. He glanced at Oscar, who was staring out the window at the passing cars, his hand pressed against his head. The gush of blood from the laceration appeared to be slowing.

Probably just a flesh wound. He'll be in good form in no time.

Robicheaux's plan to draw the woman assassin out was still viable. He fully expected her to exploit the perceived weakness he'd created in his security protocols, although he might have to tweak things a bit in order to lure her in. His mole in Russian intelligence left little doubt that she was the one they would use.

The clumsy attempt on his life already pushed to the furthest recesses of his mind, the Frenchman smiled and leaned back in his seat.

Come to me, little cat. I have something special planned for you...

CHAPTER 11

"**M**AKE THE CALL," Leine said, and handed the phone to Ilya. He stared out the window of the restaurant, his expression unreadable. They'd stopped inside the small café to regroup and warm up with a hot drink.

Leine leaned forward and pushed the phone across the table. "You want revenge for your uncle?" she asked, her voice low. There weren't many customers in the dimly lit room—a couple near the back and an old man sipping tea with a book open in front of him near the kitchen—but the less attention, the better.

Ilya had given her a terse version of what happened to his Uncle Piotr at the hands of the Frenchman and how Robicheaux left Ilya alive to spread the story after the massacre. In addition to a deep sense of survivor guilt, his anger was a palpable blaze, the idea of exacting revenge for his uncle's death the only oxygen needed to fan the flames. It was Leine's job to exploit that need and use his contacts to track down her target.

"Make. The. Call."

Ilya closed his eyes and shook his head. "I will have to tell them I failed."

"They'll find out sooner or later. And now you have me on your side."

He opened his eyes, and the corners of his mouth pulled up in a smirk. "But you are a woman," he said with a dismissive wave of his hand.

Leine let the comment slide. She shrugged. "If you don't want my help…" Her voice trailed off, and she reached for the phone. Ilya placed his hand over hers.

"Wait." He sighed. "I will make the call."

Leine released the phone, and Ilya flipped it open. He scrolled through his contacts until he found the number he was looking for, and brought the cell to his ear.

"Be sure you don't mention anything about me. Certainly don't want them to think you need a mere woman to help you carry out a man's job, right?"

Ilya glared at her. Leine stifled a smile.

"It's me," he said and sat straighter. He listened for a moment and then shook his head as though the person he was speaking with could see him. "No. I was unable to identify him. He was not there." Listening again, he grew quiet and shifted in his seat, his face turning a deep red.

Leine drummed her fingers on the table and sipped her tea. Enough time had been wasted. The Frenchman was probably on a flight to somewhere else by now. If Ilya's contact couldn't help them find Robicheaux, then she'd be forced to call Eric to see if he had any fresh intel. Something she did not want to do in light of the circumstances. His suggestion to hit Robicheaux from inside the café had been suspect to start. He rarely told her how to do her job. The last time he did was Glushenko. Both times she could have easily been killed.

She pulled out her phone and checked to see if Carlos had left a message. He hadn't. Why would Eric hang him out to dry unless he suspected something? If he did, then Eric would naturally have doubts about her. Guilt by association.

Ilya disconnected the call and pocketed the phone. "Well?"

The young Russian paused a moment, as though wrestling with whether he should trust his new ally. Finally, he gave a small nod.

"I have an address."

Leine tried calling Spartacus again but there was no answer. His shop was on the way to where the Frenchman was purported to have gone, and she'd called him from the restaurant to see if her passport was ready. As luck would have it, Sparky was still at the store and had just finished. She was welcome to pick it up as long as she arrived before midnight, at which time he would close for the evening. When she mentioned that she'd left the rifle on the roof of a building several blocks away, he assured her that none of the weapons or ammunition he provided were remotely traceable.

They walked to the front door, and Leine rang the buzzer. There was no answer, so she knocked. Still no answer.

"Maybe he left it unlocked." Ilya pushed on the glass. Surprisingly, it opened. They continued down the hallway toward the back of the building. The door to the bookstore was slightly ajar.

"Let me go first," Leine said as she reached behind her and withdrew her gun. Sparky may have left the door open because he was expecting them, but she wasn't going to take any chances. Ilya stepped back and she entered the store.

The front room looked as it did earlier that day, except three of the towering stacks of books had toppled over. Dozens of loose sheets splayed across the floor, giving the already cluttered shop an even more disorganized appearance.

A struggle?

Ilya swiveled his head, trying to take it all in. "Who does this?" he muttered under his breath.

As they moved past the scattered books, Leine stopped. Ilya gave her a questioning look, and she nodded toward the floor. One of the loose sheets bore a partial bloody footprint. She turned to survey the path leading to the outside door.

There. What she'd missed at first glance: faint, bloody footprints bearing the same design, headed in the direction of the door and fading with each step.

Careful to avoid disturbing any evidence, Leine advanced, gun first, to the brass lamp next to the bookcase where the secret room was located. She gestured to Ilya to stand aside and pressed the hidden button.

The bookcase slid open to reveal a ransacked room. Drawers had been emptied and cast aside, artwork torn from the walls and thrown to the floor, protective glass shattered, papers and files strewn across the room. The neat stacks of blank passports were gone, along with Sparky's collection of stamps.

Determining no immediate threat, Leine slid her gun into her waistband and stepped around the counter. Spartacus lay sprawled on his back with his eyes wide open and mouth agape, a jagged gash across his throat. Blood puddled on the floor beside him.

Leine crouched next to him and closed his eyes. His face had a waxy appearance, and his skin was ice cold.

"He's been dead a while."

Hands shaking, Ilya stared at the body, his face ashen. "Do you think the killer is still outside?"

Leine shook her head. "Doubtful. They accomplished what they came for." She scanned the room, her gaze landing on the closet near the back. Its door yawned open, revealing the now-empty interior. She patted down the body before rolling Spartacus onto his side to check his pockets for keys or anything else the killer may have missed, hoping to find the passport he'd made for her. A key ring with two keys was all she found: one had the BMW logo across the fob and the other looked like a generic door key, which she assumed was for the front door of the shop. She rose to her feet and made her way over to the closet, pausing to examine the space. Ilya joined her.

"There is nothing inside," he remarked unnecessarily. Leine stepped over the mess on the floor and slid her hands along the closet's back wall.

"There's a trick to opening the rear compartment, but I didn't watch him do it."

Ilya joined her in the search, running his fingers over the exposed trim, his earlier fear apparently forgotten.

That's good. He'll be much easier to work with if he's calm.

"What are we looking for?" he asked.

"Something, anything that seems unusual, like a piece of trim that moves, or a depression in the plaster. I'm not exactly sure."

They continued to feel their way along, eventually meeting in the middle.

"Are you certain there is a hidden compartment here?" Ilya asked, a look of disbelief replacing his curiosity.

Leine nodded. She frowned at the ceiling but saw nothing out of the ordinary. A slight depression in the wall just above eye level caught her attention. When she stepped closer to see it better, there was a loud click.

They both looked down. At the same time the back section of the closet moved, revealing a gap in the corner.

"Bingo," Leine breathed.

She gave the wall a push and the gap widened. Inside was another, larger space with dozens of boxes stacked floor to ceiling. A gun rack ran the length of one wall and contained an assortment of weapons—rifles, AK-47s, Mac-10s, and MP5s—and another display case containing several different types of semiautomatic pistols, including Glocks, Sig Sauers, Rugers, and Walthers. Leine peered into an open box to her left—hand grenades and flashbangs were nestled inside. Stacks of ammunition graced another.

Ilya whistled. He walked to the rack and took down an MP5, testing its heft.

"Now, this is an arsenal."

"Sparky liked to anticipate his clients." Leine proceeded to fill her pockets with ammo, hand grenades, and a flashbang.

Ilya stared at her. "Who *are* you?"

"The person who's going to help you avenge your uncle."

Ilya shook his head. "If you say so," he muttered and set the MP5 aside.

"Grab what you can safely conceal under your clothing. We'll take his car. I know where he parks."

Ilya peered into an open box next to him and reached inside.

"What about these?" he asked, handing her a bundle of passports held together with rubber bands.

Leine flipped through them, stopping midway through the stack. Each of them had a photograph already affixed to the first page. A few she recognized as fellow operatives from the Agency. She scanned through the rest before she found one with her picture and the name Ava Brentwood. She removed the passport from the bundle and checked that it had been stamped. Everything appeared legitimate.

Why did he make me wait for a passport when he already had one with my picture? It was possible that he kept several backups on hand for whenever the Agency or his other regular customers required additional identification with a quick turnaround.

Damn. Always a step ahead. Memories of past jobs flooded back, and she closed her eyes for a moment. Pushing the grief of losing a friend to the back of her mind, she returned to the task at hand, adding her fellow operatives' passports to her growing pile in case the police found the hidden room. She'd destroy them later.

They loaded up with what weapons and equipment they could carry—including two handheld radios, Kevlar vests, and a length of rope—and left the secret room. Leine closed the hidden door and they exited the shop and the building, heading down the walkway toward a side street.

The road was dark and deserted. Leine checked her watch. Eleven thirty. Unsure exactly where the sedan was parked, she pressed a button on the key fob. Halfway up the block a pair of hazard lights flashed.

"There it is," Leine said, nodding at Sparky's BMW 3-series sedan. They hurried to the car, and Leine opened the trunk, where they deposited their weapons. She shrugged off her coat and covered them, making sure to keep the nine millimeter handy, and noted that Sparky had a first aid kit. Hopefully they wouldn't need it.

"We have to make one more stop," Ilya said as he got in the passenger seat.

"You mean the address your contact gave you?"

"No. Another place, close by. There's a package."

"And what's in this package?" she asked.

Ilya stared out the windshield. "Something that may help."

"More explosives, I take it."

Ilya remained silent, his lips set in a stubborn line.

"Fine." Leine was too tired to argue. *What the hell,* she thought. *The more the merrier.*

Five minutes later, they were on their way to the Red Light District.

CHAPTER 12

L EINE SCORED A parking spot next to a canal in the Red Light District and Ilya hopped out.

"I'll be right back," he said, and disappeared down the street. Since he refused to give her the address where the Frenchman was supposedly staying, Leine had made him leave his phone, wallet, passport, and jacket in the car as proof that he would return. She stopped short of having him leave his shoes. It *was* cold.

Red and purple neon lights reflected in the inky black water of the canal. Groups of tourists huddled next to glass windows, jostling each other to catch a glimpse of the sex workers. Leine glanced at her watch. Almost midnight. The adrenaline surge she'd experienced when she found Sparky's body had ebbed, leaving her drained. The persistent thought of a good night's sleep was never far from her mind. Nearby, a restaurant window boasted a neon cup with steam coming out of the top. *Perhaps a cup of coffee would do the trick.* The restaurant's window would provide a good view of the car in case Ilya brought back any "friends" or tried something funny. She got out, locked the doors, and went inside.

As Leine waited for her espresso, she stood near the front window to keep the car in view. A short time later, Ilya returned carrying a package. He tried the passenger side door, but when he realized it was locked, he leaned against the car to wait. He appeared to be alone. A moment later, the barista called to Leine that her drink was ready. She walked to the counter to pay and waited as the woman gave her change back.

To-go cup in hand, she returned to the car. Ilya was lying on the hood with the package next to him, his head back and mouth open, snoring loudly.

She opened the driver's side door and slammed it closed. He snapped awake with a snort.

"Wha's happening?" Bleary-eyed, he glanced around, obviously trying to remember where he was.

"You're in Amsterdam. You did a shit job blowing up an arms dealer, and I'm here to help."

"Oh, yes." He nodded, his cheeks darkening in the neon light.

"Is that what I think it is?" she asked, gesturing toward the package beside him.

He picked it up as he slid off the hood and got in the car without answering her. Leine joined him inside and shoved the keys in the ignition. He leaned over and pushed the package underneath his seat.

"You mean to tell me that you left a package of explosives sitting out in the open while you decided to take a nap in the middle of Tourist Central?" Leine shook her head in disbelief.

Ilya rubbed his hands over his knees and looked down at his shoes. "Well, I—um, not exactly—"

"You should have had one of these goddamned neon lights over your head, flashing 'Free explosives here.'" She looked out the window in an attempt to calm down. It wasn't working. Leine's blood boiled. Sleep deprivation, doubts about her boss, and having to deal with a careless, irresponsible juvenile delinquent who would probably get her killed wasn't a good combination.

"Or maybe you could just hand it to a passing tourist. Great story, right?" She gripped the steering wheel. What the hell was she doing with this idiot? She was a professional. She knew how to get the address.

He'd probably cave within minutes.

Back off, Leine. He's just a kid.

Ilya cleared his throat and continued to stare at his shoes. It looked like he was on the verge of tears.

You're not cut out for this, Ilya, Leine thought. It had been a strange night. He fucked up an assassination attempt by missing his target and killing several innocent people. If that weren't enough to mess with his head, he also had to confess the debacle to his uncle's friend, who was probably some ranking member of the Russian mafia. To top it all off, a woman he didn't even know just dressed him down for his boneheaded move.

She would have to figure a way to keep him busy while she took care of Robicheaux.

"Seriously, Ilya, you need to think about this. We're heading into some dangerous territory. One mistake, one stupid move, and you could get us both killed. You know," she continued, "you *could* just give me the address and let me do my job. That way, you can live to tell your uncle's friend you took care of the Frenchman, and then he can pay you, or whatever it is you're doing this for. I won't say a word. Scout's honor." She held up two fingers, but the reference went over his head.

"What do you mean, 'let you do your job'?"

"I'm not new to the game, Ilya, and I've never had to blow anything up to complete a mission." She nodded at her handgun. "There are cleaner ways to accomplish the same objective. Not to mention safer, with a much lower mortality rate."

Ilya's eyes grew wide, his expression bordering on incredulous. "You cannot be—you are an assassin?"

She gave him a look. A frown flitted across his features, consternation obvious in his eyes. Her patience wearing thin, Leine waited as he struggled with this new information. A few moments later, he lifted his head to meet her gaze.

"I apologize. I did not know you did such a thing for a living. In my country, women don't usually—" He cleared his throat and straightened in his seat. "Of course, I should have known this. I am yours to instruct."

Leine studied the young Russian for a moment. He gave the impression of sincerity, but she'd have to watch him. Sighing inwardly, she resigned herself to dragging him along. At least he was comfortable around weapons, having grown up with an uncle who dealt in small arms.

"You're not ready for a job like this, Ilya. That much is obvious. You have to let me do what I do. I promise you that your uncle's friend will be none the wiser."

A muscle in his jaw twitched. "No. I must do this. I, Ilya Pasternak Kovshevnikov, must avenge my uncle's death." Tears shone in his eyes. He gave them a savage swipe with the back of his hand.

Shaking her head, Leine pulled back onto the street and headed east.

The job had just become infinitely more complicated.

Leine used the sedan's GPS to guide her onto the road leading to the North Sea. The temperature outside was cold but not freezing, and the roads were dry. Several kilometers and three turns later, Ilya instructed her to stop. She cut the lights and pulled off the road, concealing the car in a group of trees. They were across from a fenced lot surrounding several warehouses built on a wharf near the banks of a dark waterway. A dense fog had settled over the area, partially obscuring the buildings. There were no streetlights.

Stashing both her agency and Spartacus's cell phones and several euros under the seat, she exited the BMW. She scanned the deserted road in both directions. Nothing moved. The air itself felt as though it had paused for breath. Ilya joined her, glancing furtively left and right.

"What is this place?" he asked, his voice just above a whisper.

She drew her gun and pivoted, noting the weeds growing through asphalt beyond the chain link fence.

"Not sure. The buildings look like they haven't been used in years."

Ilya shivered and pulled his jacket tight. "But this is the address." He shoved his hands in his pockets.

Leine walked to the trunk and returned a moment later carrying an MP5 with a night scope and suppressor attached, a pair of binoculars, one of the Kevlar vests, and the two handheld radios, one of which she handed to Ilya. In addition, she'd stuffed a flashbang into her jacket pocket.

"Wait here. I'm going to see if I can find anything that will lead us to Robicheaux. There must be a reason your uncle's friend gave you this address." Leine shrugged on the vest and zipped up her coat—it barely fit over the Kevlar. *At least it's not raining.* Cold she could do. Wet she could stand. But cold and wet was a thoroughly shitty combination.

"Key the mic once for yes, twice for no, and one long followed by a short to let me know if we have company."

Ilya nodded that he understood. "You will come back for me, yes?"

"Sure, Ilya. Just make sure to stay out of sight, especially if someone drives by."

"We should sneak into the building to see if Robicheaux is inside," he insisted. Something silver glinted in the darkness. A knife. "Then I will slit his throat and watch him bleed."

"No, you won't." Her tone brooked no argument. "Wait here to see if there are any gunmen patrolling the grounds. You're not to leave this car at any time."

Ilya opened his mouth to say something, but Leine shook her head.

"I need you here in case things go sideways." If the Frenchman was somewhere nearby, she couldn't risk having Ilya blunder into the operation. He'd put them both in danger. "It's better if I go in alone to see how many men we're up against. Once I've done the reconnaissance, I'll contact you via radio. The first series of clicks you hear will be the number of guards. The second will be whether I've found Robicheaux. If he's there, I will subdue the guards and call you on the radio."

"So I can kill him," Ilya said, his eyes gleaming.

She ignored his comment. Leine had no intention of notifying him if she found Robicheaux, but he might stay put if he thought that was what she was going to do. "Do we have a deal?" Leine held out her hand.

Ilya nodded as they shook. "Then I will blow up the evidence, yes?" He gestured toward the car. "There is enough C-4 in the package to blow the hell out of any building."

"Then what? There's an art to setting explosives, the knowledge of which you clearly don't possess." A picture of the man she killed in Mexico flashed through her mind. "The noise alone will bring everyone in the vicinity to see what happened, including local law enforcement. What's your escape plan in case that happens?"

Ilya crossed his arms. "Fine. What is your idea?"

"Like I said before, I need you to be my point man."

"What is this point man?" Ilya's eyebrows knitted together.

Leine stifled the inclination to grab him by the throat and in an even voice said, "That means exactly what I just said. Stay here with the radio and warn me if you see anyone else." She handed him the set of binoculars. "I work better alone. If I find Robicheaux, like I said, I'll call you on the radio."

"No," he said, an insolent expression on his face. "I will come with you."

Leine's face warmed, her anger rising. *You have no idea how close you are to dead, kid.*

"Sorry, Ilya, that's just not going to happen. Now, you can either be my lookout, which, by the way, is an important job, or you won't be a part of this at all."

Ilya lifted his chin. "And how will you stop me?" he asked, widening his stance.

The young Russian was on the ground in less than a second. Leine put pressure on his ulnar nerve, and the knife fell from his grasp. Keeping her knee on his back, she removed a length of rope from her pocket and tied his wrists together. Then she ran the rope to his feet and tied his ankles.

"I am sorry," Ilya managed, lifting his head so his face wouldn't be crushed in the dirt. "Please let me go. I will do as you say."

Testing the knots once more, Leine stood, walked to the back of the car, and opened the trunk. She stuffed as much of the equipment as she could into the pack and transferred it to the backseat. Back at the trunk, she removed the items that hadn't fit, and hid everything behind a tree.

"You must let me go. I have learned my lesson. I will do as you say." His voice caught.

She walked back and grabbed him underneath his arms, dragging him to the rear of the car before she pulled him to his feet.

"Wait, no—I can't go in there—" His eyes bulged at the sight of the open trunk, and he pulled back, shaking his head. "I will die." The last sentence came out small and quiet.

"Sorry, Ilya. I can't take the chance that you'll fuck things up."

Ilya wriggled and thrashed his head back and forth as she shoved him into the trunk.

"No—you cannot do this to me!" Ilya's voice carried over the still night air. Leine reached inside her coat pocket for the remaining rope and cut a length with the knife. She wadded a rag Spartacus had left in the trunk and stuffed it into his mouth, secured it with the rope, and then closed the lid. The trunk vibrated with angry thudding and muffled Russian curses.

Leine leaned in close and said in a low voice, "I'm leaving now. If you continue this childishness, it's only a matter of time before Robicheaux's men find you. When that happens, they will torture you to find out what you know, which will obviously compromise the mission.

Then, once they've gotten all they can from you—and I promise, it will be quite painful—they'll kill you. I doubt very much that your uncle's friend will be impressed. What do you think?"

Silence.

Fairly sure the young idiot wouldn't draw attention to himself, Leine sprinted across the road and skirted the fence until she came to a gap large enough to squeeze through. She wished she hadn't left the rifle on the roof back in Amsterdam. She could have set up somewhere nearby and waited the Frenchman out.

Other than water lapping against the nearby dock, her measured breathing was the only sound. When she reached the side of the first building, she paused and peered through the night scope. The eerie green setting showed no life—only forgotten, rust-scarred equipment piled high in a makeshift junkyard.

She continued, pausing to listen as she did. She'd made it as far as the warehouse nearest the wharf when a faint clang echoed to her right. The fog had dissipated somewhat, revealing the shadowy outline of a ship moored next to the dock. Crouched low, she crept forward, eyes trained on the fishing trawler. The wheelhouse was located aft, with twin beams amidships. There was no light coming from the bridge.

The clang sounded again. She soon located the source: an unsecured winch swung back and forth, slamming against the boom.

She crossed the dark expanse between the warehouse and the wharf and was about to step onto the dock when rocks skittered behind her.

CHAPTER 13

LEINE MELTED INTO the shadows. Moments later, footsteps crunched on gravel, growing louder. A man carrying a machine gun over his shoulder materialized, continued onto the dock, and climbed on board the ship.

From the looks of his weapon, Robicheaux's gunmen didn't use suppressors. If they exchanged fire it would get loud, necessitating a quick escape. She paused a few moments longer. When no one else appeared, she made her way to the boat.

Except for the occasional clang of the winch, there was no activity. No voices floated toward her, which seemed odd. Water was a great conductor of sound. Curious, Leine waited a beat before she continued up the gangway and stepped onto the deck.

She noted movement in her periphery and slipped behind a large net. The man with the gun who'd passed her before came into view, slowly patrolling above decks. He stopped and reached inside his jacket for a pack of cigarettes, shook one out, and lit up. The ember glowed as he took a drag and expelled a cloud of blue smoke into the air. She waited until he turned away and then slipped up behind him with her knife.

A soft gurgle escaped his throat as blood spilled down his chest. Carefully, she lowered him to the deck and covered him with some rope. She sheathed the knife and slipped along the starboard side of the ship toward the bridge. It looked as though Robicheaux only had the one guard patrolling the upper deck. She continued along the lower section of the bridge until she came to a door.

Easing it open she listened, her breathing shallow. The faint sound of voices floated up from below, and she stepped inside, closing the door behind her.

A soft light glowed in the darkness, illuminating a set of steep metal stairs leading below decks. MP5 leading the way, she descended. At the bottom, she scanned for company but saw no one. She continued toward the voices, which she identified as male. Drawing closer, a French accent became discernible.

Her back against the wall, she inched closer to an open doorway. She could make out three distinct voices—two French speakers and one other with an indeterminate accent.

"Have they identified the bomber?" one of them demanded, obviously angry. Leine assumed the voice belonged to Robicheaux.

"No. Our contact was as surprised as we were," a deep voice replied. "The Russians lost one of their best operatives in the blast."

"And we almost lost you," said the Frenchman. There was a pause. "Set up a meeting. I need aircraft. The shipment to Liberia is in danger of being canceled, and you know what that means." The man's voice dripped with menace. "Oscar, I want you to find out who placed the explosive in the café and deal with them accordingly, no matter the cost."

"I would consider it an honor."

Leine moved to the other side of the doorway. She could use the element of surprise and enter the room now to take them all out. This appealed to her impatience to get back to the States so she could find out what had happened to Carlos, but she didn't know how many guards were in the room or on the ship, and she hadn't positively identified the Frenchman.

As she weighed her options, the door at the top of the stairwell banged open. There was a short scuffle before heavy footsteps descended the stairs. Leine slipped into a dark room opposite the stairwell as a man with a gun appeared, dragging someone behind him.

Ilya.

Shit. How'd the little idiot get caught?

The man shoved the young Russian ahead of him, hastening his progress by jabbing him in the back with his gun barrel. His hands were still tied, but the rope binding his ankles had been cut, allowing him to walk. Leine caught a glimpse of Ilya's bruised and battered face before he disappeared through the doorway. One eye had swollen shut.

What the hell? Leine had locked the car. She doubted Ilya would be stupid enough to make noise if he heard someone nearby.

Or would he?

"Who have we here?" the one she thought of as Robicheaux asked.

Ilya didn't answer.

"I heard loud thumping coming from the grove of trees across the road. He was inside the trunk of a car. He'd kicked out the backseat. Look what else I found."

"Hmm. What would such a young man be planning to do with a cache of weapons, do you think?"

A muscle in Leine's eye spasmed. Apparently they found the pack Leine had left on the back floor of the BMW.

"Do I know you?" the Frenchman said. "You seem familiar."

The man's question gave Leine more reason to believe Robicheaux was in the room. *Don't say anything, Ilya.* It would do no good to remind the Frenchman of who he was.

The Russian's capture complicated things. Ilya wouldn't hold out long when it came to the Frenchman's interrogation techniques. In fact, she was certain her presence would be compromised within minutes of Robicheaux's first attempt at retrieving information. Her choices had just narrowed considerably. Now, Ilya would most certainly be caught in the crossfire. As annoying as he was, she didn't relish the idea of killing the kid.

Time to move.

Leine sprinted along the passageway, forward past the fish hold, searching for the battery panel. She found the switch box on her second circuit. The battery on-off switch was the kind that required a T-handle to operate. Counting the seconds, Leine scanned the floor and checked between the batteries with no luck. She was about to jury-rig something else to force it when she noticed a metal tool-box pushed into a corner several feet way. She walked over to it and lifted the lid. The T-handle was inside. She returned to the battery panel, inserted the handle, and threw the switch.

Everything went black. The constant hum of the ship's engine seemed to increase in decibels. Leine waited a moment in case a backup generator kicked on. Satisfied there wasn't one, she removed the T-handle and slid it out of sight before navigating back toward the ship's stern.

Footsteps pounded toward her, echoing the length of the corridor. The erratic beam of a flashlight bounced wildly in the dark. Leine stepped into a recessed doorway and flattened herself against the wall. The gunman hurried past, focused on the corridor ahead of him. Once he cleared her location, Leine stepped into the passageway and shot him twice in the back of the head. He crumpled to the deck. She relieved him of his weapon and hurried toward the stern, using the night scope on the MP5 to find her way.

As she neared the stairs leading to the upper deck, Ilya's muffled cries erupted from the room where they'd taken him. She didn't have much time.

Neither did Ilya.

Leine fished the flashbang from her jacket, pulled the pin, and tossed it inside the door. A second later it detonated and she moved inside, keeping low and sweeping the room with the MP5. Two guards flanked Ilya, who was tied to a chair. From a crouch, Leine fired through the smoke, killing one. His hearing and sight compromised, the other gunman fired blind. A stream of bullets peppered the metal wall above her head, pinging wildly. She returned fire, shooting the second guard in the chest. His gun dropped from his grasp, clattering to the floor as he slid down the wall.

She raced across the room to Ilya.

"It's me," she said. Unsheathing the knife, she bent down and sawed through the rope holding him to the chair. She removed his gag and pulled him to his feet.

"Where's Robicheaux?" she asked.

"On the bridge," Ilya replied. "They have the passports," he added.

She picked up one of the dead guard's AK-47s and handed it to Ilya. "Here," she said as she led him to the door. She stopped to scan the passageway and stairs.

A man descended the stairwell and Leine fired. The body toppled forward but jerked to a stop near the last step, his arm wedged in the railing.

"Climb, but watch the door at the top," Leine instructed, and gave him a push. Ilya did as he was told, and Leine followed him up the stairs backward, sweeping the passageway below. Once they reached the door, she took first position and inched the door open. The upper deck and path to the gangway was clear.

"Go. I'll meet you by the car." She opened it wide enough for Ilya to slip through and then covered him as he disappeared down the walkway to the dock below.

Leine sensed someone behind her, and her body tensed for combat. She ducked and pivoted, her hand reaching for the knife.

Stars exploded behind her eyes. And the world went black.

CHAPTER 14

North Sea Trawler—location unknown

Drip.
Drip.

LEINE FOUGHT HER way back to consciousness. Her ears rang, and the back of her skull throbbed. She tried to raise her hand to rub the base of her neck but found both hands already above her, the numbness in her shoulders and arms just beginning to register. She leaned her head back and opened her eyes. Her wrists were tied with thick rope to a large metal hook hanging from a chain attached to the ceiling. She glanced at her feet. Her ankles were tied together, and her bare toes struggled to touch the floor as she tried to find purchase.

What the hell?

Icy water hit her face and she inhaled sharply, sputtering at the shock of cold.

"*Fuck.*" She shook her head and blinked the water from her eyes.

A giant of a man with a thick bandage on the side of his head and deep scars on his face stood in front of her in the stark, cold glow of a wall-mounted light, his expression bland.

The man from the café bombing.

The lone bulb on the back wall had a wire cage around it, and the greasy smell of diesel and oil were prevalent, telling her she was most likely still on the trawler. Dull gray paint covered the floor and halfway up the wall, abruptly changing to a dirty off-white. Rust poked through the paint in several places.

Conscious now, the past twenty-four hours came back to her in a confusing rush of images and smells: the acrid smoke and sickening odor of burned bodies and melted plastic from the café bombing; Spartacus lying on the floor of his secret room in a pool of his own blood; tourists jockeying for position at the window in the Red Light District and the innocuous-looking package of explosives; Ilya's beaten and bruised face; the gunmen on the trawler.

An involuntary shiver shook her, and she looked down at her bare legs. At least they left her panties on. Her shirt wasn't doing her much good even for modesty's sake—she was soaked to the skin. Her jacket, pants, and shoes lay in a heap in the corner of the steel-walled room.

The man with the scars walked to a console sitting on a rolling metal table and fiddled with the knobs. He then picked up two long wires with alligator clips on each end and approached her.

Not good.

Steeling herself for what would come next, Leine grimaced as he squeezed open one of the clips and clamped it over her shirt onto her left nipple and then did the same with the other to the right. She sucked in a breath as pain lanced through her.

"You know," she said, forcing herself to speak in an even tone, "people pay a lot of money for this." She managed to smile.

The man ignored her as he tweaked the clips. She gasped as pain spiked through her.

And this wasn't even the main event.

"Look, you won't get anything out of me that I wouldn't voluntarily give you anyway. Really." Leine tried to catch his gaze. "Ask me anything. I'll tell you whatever you want to know."

Scarface stepped back and raised his eyes to hers.

"We know who you are, that you were sent to kill the Frenchman." He smiled, revealing perfect white teeth— oddly discomfiting when viewed with his scar-ravaged face. "There is nothing further we need from you." He walked back to the console. A jolt of electricity seared through her. Leine clamped her teeth together as her body convulsed like a marionette on crack.

A few agonizing moments later, he shut it down. A wave of relief coursed through her followed by a deep, wretched aching in her shoulders and wrists.

Play for time, Leine. Dying this way will take a while.

"So," she said, gasping, "where's Robicheaux? I'm sure he doesn't want to miss this."

At that moment, the steel door at the back of the room swung open and a man with a goatee walked in wearing perfectly tailored slacks and an expensive shirt. Wiry of build, he was light on his feet and moved with purpose. What he lacked in stature he more than made up for in intensity.

He came to stand next to the much larger Scarface and patted the giant on the arm.

"I see you have met Oscar." He smiled at his henchman and then returned his attention to Leine. "I asked him to begin our little session before I arrived. A sort of a pre-torture, you know?" He ambled closer to Leine and circled her slowly.

"I must say, I am disappointed. When I'd heard that they were sending the *Léopard* to kill me I imagined a feral, terribly dangerous she-cat." He brought his hands up and clawed the air. "Rawr." He snorted. "Obviously, I've been misinformed, because to look at you now you are nothing—a *petite chatte*—a little pussy, *oui*?"

His laughter echoed off the walls as he twirled his index finger mid-air. "Oscar."

This time the jolt lasted longer and was far more robust. Leine fought against it but soon lost consciousness. The ice water revived her, but when she tried to lift her head, her neck muscles refused to obey. Robicheaux drew closer and wrapped his hand around her chin in a savage grip, then forced her head up to look at him. His eyes flashed with anger.

"And the bomb at the café?" He shook his head. "Really, mademoiselle. Such amateur work. I expected better."

He let go and her head dropped. "I need a strong adversary. One who will challenge me. One I can proudly say I vanquished. Not this—this sad excuse for an assassin."

The temporary paralysis began to subside. Leine lifted her head a fraction of an inch. Robicheaux snapped his fingers, and Oscar rolled the cart with the console over to him.

The Frenchman picked up a long knife that was sitting on the table and turned to Leine.

"Unless, of course, you didn't plant the bomb that almost killed my friend." He ran his thumb across the blade, testing its sharpness. "I've heard that the Russian mafia tattoo members who fail to live up to expectations.

I thought it only fair that you suffer the same consequences. A quick death seems so—" Robicheaux looked at the ceiling as though searching for the right word, "—unfair to those who don't pull their weight. And you, *mon amie*, have most certainly *not* pulled your weight. I barely needed one bodyguard, let alone a security team as your reputation suggested." He sighed and shook his head. "I relished having a professional with which to play this game. A chance to sharpen my claws. Oh." He covered a smile with his hand. "There it is again. I have referenced felines."

Oscar walked behind her and wrapped his arms around her thighs as Robicheaux slid the knife beneath the lowest button on her shirt. He flicked the blade and the button flew off, skipping across the cement floor. Using the tip, he folded back the two sides of her shirt, exposing her midriff. Leine concentrated on the far wall, willing herself to relax.

At first the blade stung, but the Frenchman continued carving into her skin, and the pain intensified. Oscar's body heat was matched only by the warm blood running down her abdomen from the cuts Robicheaux made. Leine forced herself to compartmentalize the pain, to isolate it, reducing its effect on her. She continued to breathe deeply, her eyes glued to a dark spot on the wall, convincing her body to ignore what was happening. Perspiration spilled down the sides of her face.

Mind over matter, Leine. If you don't mind, it doesn't matter.

The Frenchman paused and rolled up his sleeve, revealing the tattoo of a guillotine on his right bicep. He reached behind him on the console for a small plastic cup and glanced up at her. "You see, I am known for this, *la guillotine*. The obvious meaning is because I am French

109

and am known to execute those in my way. But there is a little more to the story."

He wiped at the blood on her abdomen and proceeded to fill the cuts with blue ink from the plastic cup in his hand.

"When I was a child, my father used to beat my mother in front of me. He told me it was the way of men and that I should learn from his actions." He paused to study his handiwork before continuing. "And I did learn, but it wasn't what he'd intended. One night, after a particularly vicious beating that left my mother unable to talk, I waited until he'd fallen asleep in his chair from too much drink and slit his throat. Then I chopped off his head with a cleaver. It was very sharp, a blade like a guillotine." He slid his finger across his throat and smiled. Robicheaux put the cup of ink back on the table and admired his work.

"As you see, I have given you your own tattoo, letting all who see your body know your failure as an assassin. It says Emile. My name. Now everyone will know I vanquished the *Léopard*. Not that it was difficult," he added.

Leine's anger rose, allowing her to blot out the pain. She ground her teeth and imagined her legs wrapped around his head, snapping his neck.

Robicheaux closed one eye, again studying his handiwork. Then he reached behind him for a plastic bottle on the console. He opened the top and poured its contents over the cuts, allowing the liquid to spill down her body. As the burning registered, Leine chewed her lip to keep from crying out. The Frenchman smiled.

"We mustn't let it get infected." He set the bottle of rubbing alcohol back on the table and rose from his chair.

A percussive thud sounded on the other side of the trawler, and the ship bucked violently. Thrown to the floor, Robicheaux landed on his hands and knees. Oscar lost his grip on Leine's legs and barreled toward the console. Flailing his arms, he careened past the table, which skidded across the floor after him. The wires connecting Leine to the console grew taut, and the alligator clips tore away from her nipples, ripping her shirt. She cried out as white-hot pain speared through her. The table smashed into the giant, pinning him against the wall, and he slumped sideways. Leine swung back and forth with the hook, slowing as the vessel settled.

A deafening silence followed the explosion. Robicheaux climbed to his feet and staggered toward the door.

"Fuck," he shrieked. He'd made it to the corridor when the trawler creaked loudly and pitched to one side, groaning as she tipped. The Frenchman disappeared as the door slammed closed behind him.

Summoning every last bit of strength, Leine lifted her legs and slipped the rope binding her ankles onto the hook. She worked her wrists side to side and tried to loosen the ties enough to free her hands.

The door banged open. Leine stepped up her attempts to get free. Had the Frenchman come back for her, or did Oscar regain consciousness?

She twisted to look over her shoulder. Eyes wide, Ilya scrambled on all fours toward her across the tilting deck.

"Ilya," Leine shouted, nodding toward the console. Oscar looked like he was still unconscious. "Over there. They had a knife. See if you can find it."

With difficulty, Ilya changed direction and moved to where the giant lay.

The rope around her wrists started to give, but only a little. The ship listed further. Ilya flattened himself against the wall, his face ghostly pale.

"Hurry, Ilya," Leine urged.

Using the wall for balance, he staggered to the console and rummaged through the wreckage. He looked up, shaking his head.

"There is nothing," he yelled.

"Check again," Leine said. "I know they had a knife." Ilya moved to the other side of the table.

"Yes! I found it."

"Bring it here."

Ilya scrambled toward her. She lowered her legs.

He stared at her abdomen and his eyes traveled to her breasts. "You're bleeding."

"Cut me down first. Don't worry about the wounds."

Ilya nodded and sawed through the ropes around her ankles. He glanced behind him at the rolling table wedged against Oscar.

"There's no time. With the floor tilted like this the table won't stay still long enough. You need to climb up my back."

She wrapped her hands firmly around the metal hook and crossed her legs. Ilya slid the knife into his back pocket and grabbed her shoulders. Using her legs as a step, he wrapped his knees around her waist and shimmied up her body until he could reach her wrists. Leine stifled a groan having to hold both his weight and hers while he sawed at the bindings.

"When the rope looks like it's about to break, throw the knife as far as you can so we don't land on it," she instructed. The ship creaked again.

"Okay. Almost—" Ilya hurled the knife across the room and let go of the hook. Their combined weight broke the remaining strands of rope, and they plunged to the floor. Leine's legs buckled, and she lurched sideways onto her hip, catching herself with her hands. Ilya grimaced as he landed on his arm.

"Are you all right?" Leine asked. Ilya nodded. She climbed to her feet and started for her clothes. Ilya scrambled past her and grabbed her coat and pants.

"My shoes."

He handed her the clothing and turned back for the shoes. She shrugged on her pants and jacket and checked the pockets. Her fingers closed around a wad of tissue. She pulled it free and stuffed it against her abdomen to stem the bleeding.

Ilya had almost reached her shoes when the ship shuddered and the floor shifted. Leine threw herself backward to maintain her balance. Ilya did the same. Both lost the fight and slid toward the exit, coming to rest at the base of a wall.

Her shoes rolled to a stop near the door. She crab-walked to them, and the two of them staggered to the exit.

Pausing at the door to catch her breath and pull her shoes on, she glanced back at Oscar. It was obvious from this angle that the impact had smashed the back of his head open. Streaks of blood ran down the wall, pooling on the floor.

Ilya looked at Leine, a triumphant expression on his face.

"See? The C-4 came in handy."

CHAPTER 15

USING THE HANDRAILS along the corridor, Leine and Ilya worked their way toward the ship's high side.

"Did you see Robicheaux leave the boat?" Leine asked.

Ilya shook his head. "I set the explosives on the outside of the ship's bow, near the waterline. It is possible he died in the explosion."

"He was in the room with me when your bomb went off. Disappeared out the door before you showed up."

A frown creased Ilya's forehead. "But I did not see him leave the boat with the rest of his men."

"He probably escaped when you were cutting me free."

"Then we must find him."

"First we need to get topside to see what kind of time we have until this boat sinks."

Several minutes later, they made it to the port side stairwell. The door at the head of the stairs was wide open. Leine motioned for Ilya to keep going.

"Watch your back, and make sure you're not seen. Robicheaux and his men may still be nearby."

"Aren't you coming?"

Leine shook her head. "I need to find those passports." *And make sure the Frenchman isn't onboard.*

She half expected him to insist on joining her, but clearly his sense of self-preservation won out. He stepped onto the bottom stair and grabbed hold of the handrail.

"Take the car to the outskirts of Amsterdam and get on a train. I'll find another way back." Leine handed him the keys to the BMW. "Be sure to grab the equipment I hid in the trees. Ditch the car as soon as you can and remove everything. The police may have found Spartacus's body and reported his vehicle as stolen. Wipe your prints. Don't forget the door handles and inside the trunk."

"But how will I know if the Frenchman is alive or dead?"

"If he's alive, it won't be long before you hear of him again."

Ilya paused for a moment, clearly conflicted.

"Go. It's too dangerous. Stay alive and you'll get another chance at Robicheaux."

That seemed to mollify him, and he turned back to the stairwell. She followed him to the upper deck and, after ensuring no one was visible on the ship or the dock, they parted ways. Ilya headed toward the partially submerged bow. He slid into the dark water and disappeared.

There was still time to do what she needed.

The door leading into the wheelhouse was unlocked. She peered through the window to make sure no one was inside before she entered and began to search for the passports. If they weren't there, then she'd have to find Robicheaux's quarters. She doubted he'd thought to grab them on his exit from the trawler. He didn't strike her as the type to remain long on a sinking ship. The trawler appeared stable at the moment, its lower compartments likely filling with seawater. It would only be a matter of time until the boat would list yet again. The next shift might signal the vessel's last breath.

The passports were inside a middle drawer in the center console. She pulled them out and rifled through them. They were all there, hers included. She shoved them inside her coat pocket and started for the door. Halfway onto the deck the door slammed into her, shoving her sideways against the frame. At first she thought the ship had shifted, but a hand gripped the edge of the door. The hinges groaned and the door flew open revealing Robicheaux with a gun. Without thinking, Leine dropped to a crouch and barreled into him. The gun fired and he hit the railing with a grunt. He lost his grip and his weapon fell to the deck, skittering out of sight.

Adrenaline fueling her, she pummeled him against the railing, hitting him wherever she could find an opening. Robicheaux countered the blows and pushed her back into the wheelhouse. She shifted her stance and delivered a kick to his crotch. The Frenchman doubled over with a wheeze, and Leine brought her knee up. His head snapped back and hit the door frame. Blood streamed from his nose.

Leine advanced, but Robicheaux dodged right and she overshot her mark. Exhausted but still feeling the effects of the adrenaline rush, her vision tunneled. She didn't see the gaff in the Frenchman's hand. Too late, she raised her arm to fend off the blow. There was a loud crack followed by excruciating pain.

The Frenchman pushed the gaff hard against her neck. She slid her good hand under the bar in an attempt to keep him from crushing her windpipe. Fatigue dogged her and spots appeared before her eyes as she gasped for air.

"Even your own government wants you dead," Robichueax snarled, his breath hot against her cheek.

Her left arm now useless, she let go of the gaff with her right hand and jabbed him in the throat, but misjudged the distance and only delivered a fraction of the force she'd intended. Robicheaux's expression darkened as he bore down harder.

Darkness clouded her periphery, and she thrashed her head from side to side, trying to suck air into her lungs. A flash of orange on the wall to her right caught her attention and she stretched her fingers toward it.

With her last breath, Leine ripped the flare gun off its mount, aimed it at Robicheaux and pulled the trigger. The projectile burrowed into his eye socket, his screams cut short as the chemicals ignited and seared through his brain. Smoke billowed from the gaping, bloody hole in his head, filling the wheelhouse.

Coughing and gasping, Leine turned away and staggered onto the deck as the Frenchman fell to the floor. She paused to fill her lungs with crisp, briny air and waited for the dizziness to abate.

The trawler's deck was dark, cloaking her in shadow. Holding her left arm close to her body, she lurched toward the bow, which was now completely submerged, along with most of the starboard side. Illuminated by starlight, amorphous shapes hurried along the dock as shouts filled the air.

She took a deep breath and slipped off the boat into the icy, dark water. The North Sea buoyed her to the surface and she kicked toward shore.

CHAPTER 16

MOVING FAST TO stay warm, Leine had covered some distance when a pair of headlights lit the road ahead of her. She waited out of sight in the ditch and ducked down further as the vehicle rolled past. It was the BMW. The passenger side window was open, showing Ilya behind the wheel.

Leine brought her good hand to her mouth and whistled. The brake lights came on, and the car slowed. She climbed out of the ditch, hurried to the car, and slid into the passenger seat.

"Good to see you," she said, leaning toward the warm air flowing from the vents. "Is that how they got in?" She gestured toward the wide open window.

"Yes. They broke the glass." Ilya accelerated and they sped forward.

"What the hell are you still doing here? Not that I'm unhappy about it."

"I could not leave you, not with Robicheaux's men still on the dock. What happened?" he asked, nodding at her arm.

"I found him."

Ilya's eyes widened. "Is he—"

"Dead? Yes." Leine stared through the windshield. Pink streaks were beginning to fill the pre-dawn sky.

"How did you do it?" Ilya leaned forward, his excitement and curiosity obvious.

"Flare gun." She leaned her head back and closed her eyes. "I'm going to need a doctor. I think my arm is broken. We can ditch the car then. Before that, though, I need the first aid kit for Robicheaux's little tattoo." She slid her hand over her abdomen.

"Okay."

"Did you get the equipment I stashed in the trees?"

Ilya nodded. "Yes. It's all in the back seat."

"Good. We should probably get rid of everything except the most essential items, in case we're pulled over."

Ilya parked the car on the side of the road near the waterway, and they went through the items. Leine kept the 9mm and talked Ilya out of the MP5, suggesting he also take a pistol.

"The MP5 is impossible to hide. This way you can easily dispose of your weapon if you need to."

Disappointment obvious on his face, Ilya wiped the submachine gun down. They disassembled the weapons and Ilya chucked them into the water, taking care to toss the components in different directions. Leine retrieved Spartacus's first aid kit from the trunk and returned to the passenger seat. Gingerly, she unzipped her pants and smeared ointment onto the bloody cuts, grimacing as she did. Then she opened several self-adhesive bandages and placed them over the jagged tattoo. She did the same to her nipples. Ilya got back in the car and they headed for Amsterdam.

Even with the dull ache throbbing in her forearm and open window blowing cold air in her face, the warmth from the heater and subtle rocking of the car soon coaxed Leine into an exhausted, dreamless sleep.

Sometime later, there was a tap on her shoulder. Disoriented, Leine opened her eyes.

"We're here." Ilya took the keys from the ignition, wiped them with his shirt to remove his fingerprints, and placed them on the visor.

Still groggy from the short nap, Leine glanced out the window. They were in central Amsterdam, a block down from a 24-hour emergency room. Gray shadows stretched across the street from the early morning sun.

"I owe you one." Relieved to find both phones and the stash of euros where she'd left them, she opened the door and got out, tensing at the blast of cold air on her wet clothes. A story involving a bicycle accident and a canal formed in her mind—in case the doctor was curious.

Ilya got out and stood by the car, his concern obvious. "I will stay until the doctor has seen you. You may need my help."

"Thanks, but I think it best if we part ways. You should call your uncle's friend and tell him about the Frenchman's death. Remember, you used an orange flare gun." Leine stepped onto the sidewalk. "Don't mention my involvement. If for some reason my name comes up, tell him I didn't make it. And you should probably wipe down the rest of the car for prints." She started for the hospital.

Ilya called after her. "I will not forget what you did."

Without turning around, Leine raised her good arm and waved.

Several hours later, Leine walked out of the hospital with a new cast. The gaff had fractured her ulna, but the bone hadn't broken through and she was still able to use her fingers, although her hand was far too weak for much of anything. The doctor and nurse had both been interested in her cover story, and she found herself embellishing things to a ridiculous degree, eliciting laughter from them both. It felt good to be around normal people who weren't out to kill her. Maybe if the whole assassin gig didn't work out she'd try stand-up.

Then again, probably not.

She caught a nearby tram and rode it to her hotel, stopping at the front desk for the key.

"Your husband was just here," the hotel clerk said.

Husband? "Did he leave a message?" Leine asked. *Other than Eric and Mindy, who the hell knows I'm here?*

The clerk shook her head. "I'm sorry, no. He did settle your bill, though."

"He what?"

"Paid your bill. But only through last night. I'm afraid I'll need a deposit if you're going to stay longer."

"Oh. No, I won't be staying. Would you mind if I went up to get the rest of my things?"

"There's no need. Housekeeping has already cleaned the room. There was nothing."

"Okay. Thank you. My husband must have gotten it all, then."

The clerk gave her a quizzical look. "Is everything all right?"

Leine plastered on a reassuring smile. "Everything's fine, really. Thank you for the information. If I could just get my passport, I'll be on my way."

A look of panic crossed the clerk's face. "I'm sorry. Your husband said you were in an accident and that he was to pick up your passport for you." She glanced at the cast on Leine's arm. "He had a letter with your signature giving him permission." The words trailed off, and her face grew red.

"No, no, that's fine. As you can see, there was indeed an accident." Leine lifted her cast for effect. "I must have forgotten he'd done that." She smiled an apology and shrugged. "The painkillers they give you these days."

The clerk nodded in agreement. "They can be very strong, can't they?"

"Yes, they can. Would you mind calling me a taxi?"

"Of course." Obviously relieved she wasn't in trouble for giving away Leine's passport, the clerk picked up the phone and made the call.

Leine curled her fingers around the damp passports and the gun in her coat pocket. Whoever her "husband" was had effectively made her disappear. The only people who knew the name on the passport she'd used to get into the country were Eric and Mindy, but Mindy wouldn't have left her without a way home. Obviously, this was Eric's handiwork.

And now he thought she was dead.

Ten minutes later, the taxi arrived.

"Schiphol, please," she told the driver and settled back in her seat. If Eric believed that she'd died from the bomb at the café or the Frenchman had killed her, then she had the element of surprise. She felt safe in assuming Eric wasn't privy to the name on the passport that Sparky created, so she wouldn't be flagged when she boarded her flight or when she went through customs back in the States.

If Eric was behind the attempt to eliminate her, and it certainly looked as though he was, it was going to be a challenge to find out Carlos's location. If he was still alive. She could try to enlist Mindy's help, but Leine assumed

Eric would have already informed her of Leine's untimely death. As loyal as Mindy was, there was a risk that she would alert Eric to Leine's presence in the States, even when asked not to. No, she would have to go the direct route.

The driver glanced in his rearview mirror and muttered something under his breath. Leine turned to look out the back window just as a dark SUV surged forward and slammed into them, throwing her against the front seat.

"*Merda,*" the driver yelled, and stepped on the brakes.

"No! Keep driving," Leine shouted, bracing herself.

"What? No, no. There is accident. I must stop," he replied in broken English and started to pull over.

Leine glanced at the name on his taxi license. "Nicolau—listen to me. If you stop, we will both be killed. Now move!"

Eyes wide, Nicolau visibly swallowed, gripped the steering wheel, and floored the accelerator. The taxi surged forward, followed closely by the SUV.

Leine twisted in her seat in time to see the passenger window roll down and a gun appear. She ducked as the back window shattered. Nicolau screamed and hunched low in his seat, praying aloud as he swerved wildly through traffic.

She pulled out her pistol and inched up far enough to catch a glimpse of the SUV. They were two car lengths behind but gaining. Nicolau was doing a good job of keeping them at bay, but it was only a matter of time before either traffic or circumstances slowed them.

"We need more distance," she yelled.

"I am *trying.*" Nicolau glared at her in the rearview mirror.

"If you can manage at least a block between us and the SUV, then take the next side street and let me out. I'll have time to set up, and you'll have time to get the hell out of here."

Apparently, Nicolau liked the idea. He straightened in his seat, leaned forward, and stomped on the gas. Leine managed to remain upright by bracing against the backseat with her feet on the floor. Her left arm throbbed, but she pushed the sensation away. There'd be time to deal with that later.

How did these guys track me to the hotel?

The most feasible explanation was the burner phone Sparky had given her. Her chest tightened at the thought of his betrayal.

A large delivery truck trundled into the intersection they'd just gone through, blocking the SUV's way. She reached in her pocket, removed the phone, and hurled it through the shattered window as Nicolau swerved onto a narrow side street. They flew past trees and parked cars and centuries-old buildings before turning again onto an even narrower street with several commercial-sized trash bins. It was here that Nicolau brought the taxi to an abrupt stop.

"Get this car out of sight. If they see you, they'll assume I'm still inside." Leine tossed a hundred-euro note onto the front seat and got out. Without a backward glance, Nicolau gunned it. The tires chirped as the taxi shot forward, squealed around the next corner, and disappeared.

Sliding the gun into her waistband, Leine ducked behind the closest garbage bin and waited.

She didn't think the gunmen in the SUV would be able to find her now. Not after getting rid of the phone and Nicolau's evasive driving. But she needed to be certain.

A few minutes later a car turned into the alley. Leine's heart rate skyrocketed.

She peered around the edge of the bin. The black SUV coasted slowly toward her down the narrow street. Flattening her back against the brick wall, she drew her gun. She was going to have to take them out one-handed with a pistol. *Did they just get lucky and pick the right alley?* There was no way they could still be tracking her, unless…

Leine closed her eyes. *Of course.*

The agency-issued phone.

Eric.

Balancing the gun on her knee she shoved her hand into her coat pocket and pulled out the other cell phone. Anger at her boss's betrayal swept through her. With the SUV still several meters away, she hurled the mobile into the next bin over. Then she moved behind the dumpster. Moments later, the front end of the SUV rolled into view.

The man in the passenger seat was looking ahead at the next bin and didn't notice Leine. She fired. Two rounds hit the gunman in the side of the head, and he slumped forward. His weapon fell from his grip and clattered to the ground. The driver swiveled in his seat, his weapon pointed at Leine. She fired again. He was dead before he could pull the trigger. His hand dropped. His chin hit his chest. The SUV rolled to a stop.

Leine waited in case there were more inside. When no one else appeared, she made sure both gunmen were dead, and pocketed their ammo. She didn't bother to check for identification. There was no suppressor on her gun, and the shots had echoed in the narrow alley. It wouldn't be long before someone called the police.

Still jacked up on adrenaline, she followed first one street and then another until she came to a metro stop where several people were preparing to board a tram. Leine melted into the crowd and rode the tram to the city center. There she transferred to a train going to the airport. She had to get back to the States and confront Eric.

It was a safe bet he'd be surprised to see her.

CHAPTER 17

San Francisco, California

WHAT HAPPENED TO your arm?" the man in the seat next to Leine asked.

"Cycling accident," she answered. Damn thing ached like a bitch. The doctor who set her arm had told her to curtail strenuous activity. Like that was going to happen.

"Ouch. That's tough," the guy said.

He'd tried to engage her from the moment the jet had taken off from Amsterdam, but Leine had ignored him and he gave up. She glanced out the window to watch their approach to San Francisco International. The scenery always reminded her of Italy. The dark green of the oak trees and scrub, rolling brown hills, and steel-blue ocean gave the area its distinctive Mediterranean look. It was late afternoon and the usual coastal fog had already burned off, leaving bright sunshine in its wake.

Once more, the man attempted to prompt her into a conversation but Leine continued to ignore him by gazing out the window. It didn't take long before he realized she didn't want to talk and returned to his magazine.

She'd managed a few hours of sleep on the flight from Amsterdam, even though she'd been peppered with dark dreams that wouldn't let her rest. The Frenchman's last words kept playing through her mind.

Even your own government wants you dead.

Carlos had been right. Eric was trying to kill her. After years of working for him on highly sensitive jobs and developing what she thought of as a working level of trust, the possibility that Eric was specifically targeting both her and Carlos was difficult to wrap her mind around.

Robicheaux had known she was coming. Only Eric and his Russian counterpart knew of her involvement in the operation. Eric had been monitoring her whereabouts remotely and was aware she'd survived both the café bombing and the Frenchman. Even though it would take time for news of the gunmen's deaths to reach him, alerting him to her survival, she had to play it like Eric was already aware she was still alive.

Shards of worry etched her mind. Their own boss was targeting them both.

Carlos was missing.

What had Eric done?

Exhausted as she was, incendiary anger at her boss burned through her, giving her clarity and purpose. As soon as the plane landed, she caught a cab to the Tenderloin and Carlos's place.

Half-expecting to see him, she took the stairs two at a time. The door had been left partially open. Heart thudding, she paused to listen before entering. Not hearing any activity, she eased into the apartment.

Kitchen cupboards gaped open, their fragile contents smashed on top of the granite counters and across the floor. The door to the refrigerator was ajar. Whatever food had been left on the shelves now trailed along the tile. Stuffing exploded from jagged cuts in the couch cushions and throw pillows. Carlos's collection of movies had been ripped apart and the DVDs thrown across the room, scattered like silver fish scales.

A knot forming in the pit of her stomach, Leine moved through the chaos, headed for the bedroom. The mattress had been tipped onto the floor to give access to the frame, a jagged slice splitting the entire length and width. The painting Carlos purchased in Hong Kong lay on the floor beside the bed, its canvas punched through. Leine scanned the spot where it had hung, searching for the faux brick. It blended perfectly with the others around it. She climbed over the wreckage and pulled the brick free, shaking the key from its hiding place. Relief surged through her.

Grabbing one of Carlos's backpacks, she exited the apartment, closed the door behind her, and took the stairs to the storage room on the lower level. She found locker number nine near the back, inserted the key, and opened the door.

Inside was a loaded 9mm pistol, a large sealed envelope with the word "Razorback" hand printed on the front in black marker, two false passports with Carlos's picture, money, and a black laptop. Using her teeth, Leine ripped the top of the envelope off, revealing several photocopies and two CDs in jewel cases. Each had a date and time written on them. She stuffed the laptop and the envelope inside the backpack and left the building.

She found a quiet café a few blocks from the apartment, with only one other customer occupying a table. Leine chose a booth, booted up the laptop, and slid the first CD into the tray. The waiter came over, and she ordered an espresso and biscotti. She then returned to the files on the screen.

The first file she opened was a spreadsheet simply titled *Accounts*. Each tab represented consecutive years. She clicked through the current year and skimmed the entries. There were several columns to each. The first column listed operation codenames followed by a start date, completion date, and a place for comments. The last few columns were dollar amounts. The first of these was titled *Gross*. The rest were various headings accounting for expenses, followed by a column labeled *Net*.

A typical spreadsheet keeping track of income and expenses.

She recognized several dates that corresponded with jobs she'd carried out, as well as those that Carlos had done. The bulk of expenses included the operative's payouts along with costs associated with the job such as transportation, hotel, meals, and weapons.

So far, nothing damning. The files appeared to be accounting spreadsheets for Eric's personal use. What had Carlos found that he thought would implicate Eric in using the Agency's operatives off-book? She checked the other entries but found nothing unusual.

She ejected the CD and slid in the second one.

Another spreadsheet. This one was named Razorback. Leine checked the dates and stopped at October 29, the day she'd been ambushed on the Glushenko job. The start date was correct, but the codename read like gibberish, and the completion date had a minus sign instead of the actual date she'd completed the mission. A separate entry had been added in the comments field that read, *OpS-RS*. She assumed the RS was similar to the shorthand Eric used when an op had to be rescheduled, but she wasn't sure what OS meant. The Op could mean

Operation or Operative or something else entirely, and she had no idea what the S stood for. She skimmed some of the other codenames and came to one where the operative had died in action. OpD had been typed in the comment section. Operative died?

So OpS meant Operative Survived?

Leine checked the date she'd completed the Medina job, but the entries ended the day before her trip to Campeche. Which probably meant Carlos hadn't been back to download more recent information.

Pushing away dark thoughts that threatened to derail her, she downloaded the information from both CDs to the laptop's hard drive and put them back inside the envelope. The papers turned out to be black-and-white copies of photographs taken from a distance showing Eric with various people. She stopped at a series of three pictures with the same man.

All three were taken from a high vantage point with a long lens—probably a rooftop. The first showed Eric standing next to a black limousine, shaking the other man's hand—Adrian "The Wolf" Volkov—the largest black market arms dealer in the world. In the second photograph, Volkov was handing Eric a large briefcase. The third showed Eric in the driver's seat of a different car with the case open on his lap. The case was filled with cash.

Never mind the myriad questions raised by Eric's connection to Volkov, not to mention the conflict of interest that connection represented, but Leine knew for a fact that Eric did not use currency in the Agency's transactions. Transacting business in cash was far too risky given the nature of the Agency's work. If word leaked of a payout, theft was a real threat. Not only that, but Eric usually didn't like to micro-manage his operatives, and if money was involved, there was a possibility that it might disappear in-house. Eric preferred labyrinthine offshore transfers using shell corporations within shell corporations.

Plausible deniability.

The Frenchman was Volkov's direct competitor. If Carlos's suspicions were right, then Eric's cash exchange with the arms dealer pointed to securing an illicit contract on Robicheaux's life. Volkov was rumored to be in bed with high-ranking members of the Russian government who had a huge stake in the Frenchman's death.

She thought back to Ilya and the café bombing. Eric strongly suggested she take Robicheaux out from close quarters, but Leine had nixed the idea. Had Eric somehow set in motion Ilya's ill-conceived attempt on the Frenchman's life? Ilya said he didn't know the name of his uncle's friend, but it was obvious the young Russian's contact had access to real-time information that could only come from high up within the Russian government. Or possibly the Russian mafia.

What if the friend was Volkov?

Leine slid the pictures back inside the envelope and powered down the laptop. She stood up and shrugged on her jacket, the weight of the gun reassuring. Eric had answers, of that she was certain. Her boss would need convincing.

And Leine was just the woman to do it.

CHAPTER 18

B Y THE TIME Leine arrived at Agency headquarters, she'd gotten control of her anger, replacing emotion with the calculating, pragmatic side she used in her work.

The side that won.

The elevator doors pinged open, and she stepped onto the marble floor of the reception area. On first impression the surroundings gave off a formidable law firm vibe. No sign or logo graced the wall behind the receptionist's desk—just a huge flower arrangement that was changed daily. The expensive furnishings were all dark wood and gleaming surfaces, suggesting old money and old boys.

Ignoring the receptionist's request to sign in, Leine bypassed the front desk and headed straight for Eric's corner office. When she walked through the double doors, Mindy looked up from a stack of papers on her desk, her welcoming smile replaced by a look of astonishment.

"Leine."

"Is he in?" Leine asked.

"My God, we thought you were dead…" Mindy rose from her chair and came around the desk toward her, relief etching her face. She stopped short of contact and frowned, apparently unsure of Leine's mood.

"Is he in," Leine repeated, her voice cold.

Mindy seemed flustered at the unfriendly tone but soon recovered. "He went home early. He didn't say why." She returned to the desk and picked up the phone. "He'll be so relieved you're okay."

"Put the phone down, Mindy."

Mindy glanced at Leine, wariness obvious in her eyes. After a moment's hesitation, she replaced the receiver. "Is this because of Carlos?" she asked. Her expression softened as tears glistened in her eyes. "I'm so, so sorry."

Time ground to a halt. Leine stopped mid-breath, a dense pit forming in her stomach.

"Carlos?" She took a step toward Mindy, but ice-cold dread blocked her from further progress. "What about Carlos?" she repeated, louder this time, the emotional walls she'd constructed against the inevitable collapsing around her.

Mindy's face paled and she shook her head as she moved toward her.

"I—I thought you knew," she said, her voice catching. "Oh my God, I thought you knew."

Leine allowed Mindy to guide her to a chair and she sank onto the cushions, the finality of Mindy's words searing a path through her heart. The sunlight from the window dulled, and the shadows around her seemed to deepen until there was only a pinpoint of light before her. Soon, even that disappeared. She closed her eyes against Mindy, against the agency, against Eric and everything he represented.

A moment later, Leine opened her eyes and remembered to breathe. Mindy knelt in front of her, concern evident on her face.

"Leine, are you all right?" she asked. "Please tell me you're all right." Her hands fluttered ineffectually through the air.

"I'm fine," she answered. Her voice sounded far away and hollow. Even though she had suspected the outcome, the news chilled her. Ignoring Mindy's attempts at consolation, Leine rose from the chair and started for the door, her anger at Eric shoved aside to make way for the cascade of grief threatening to overwhelm her.

"Leine, wait. Maybe this will help…" Mindy hurried to her desk and picked up a thick folder lying on top. Leine paused and waited as she carried it to her and slid it into her hand.

"It's a copy of Carlos's file. Eric asked me to archive the information, but I always make a copy for my records. I just don't trust them down there." She meant the file clerks several floors below them. "It might help to bring you peace, when you're ready. The report says he didn't suffer." Her voice softened with the last sentence.

Leine barely glanced at the file as she turned to leave. "Would you do something for me, Mindy?" she asked over her shoulder.

"Yes—anything."

"Would you not tell Eric I'm here? At least, not yet." Leine turned her head. "I need some time to myself to process this. And you know how he is. He'll expect me to go straight back to work. Thinks that's the way to get past things, and I—I just can't right now."

"Of course. This never happened. Please let me know if there's anything I can do."

Somehow, Leine made it down the hallway and took the elevator to the lobby. She exited the building and started to walk, unaware of where she was headed. She just needed to move, to escape the Agency and Eric.

Unsettling images crowded her mind, and she walked blindly, only semi-aware of the people she passed. A numbness had formed in her chest and spread to the rest of her. When she finally came back to the present, she found herself next to a bench in Crissy Field. The sun was just beginning to set, tinting the grass and casting a rose-gold hue over the orange-colored Golden Gate Bridge. Dark clouds building in the west signaled an approaching storm. Waves lapped at the bulkhead, lulling her emotions into a fragile calm.

She sat on the bench and set the folder beside her.

Carlos is dead.

The words kept coming back: *Carlos is dead.* She'd known it could happen. They both did. It added an urgency to their love for each other which otherwise might not have been. But they were invincible. At least, that's what they'd thought. So many close calls, so many injuries. Still they survived, giving them both an unreasonable expectation of living.

Together.

The sun sank lower, silhouetting a pair of lovers walking hand in hand along the edge of the breakwater, oblivious to the anguish squeezing Leine's chest. Her brain told her it was impossible for anyone to know her thoughts, but her heart couldn't believe the whole world didn't notice her pain, didn't stop to acknowledge that the man she loved was gone from her life forever.

The Golden Gate Bridge stretched across San Francisco Bay, beckoning. How many people had taken their own lives when faced with a devastating loss? Now she understood. How could she live with such pain?

Then again, how could she not? April would need her now more than ever.

Shadows stretched toward her, encasing her in darkness. One by one, lights flickered on, casting her surroundings in a harsh glow. The cold damp of early evening seeped through to her bones, and she roused herself, her gaze falling to the bench and the file Mindy had given her. She picked it up and paged through, stopping at his picture, which had been paper-clipped to the notification of his death. She stared at his handsome face, the hot prick of tears threatening to spill over at what could have been. Almost against her will, she skimmed the report. One word stopped her cold.

Campeche.

She blinked, not believing, but there it was. Unable to breathe, Leine forced herself to read further, the horrifying realization cascading through her at the impossibility.

Local authorities found the operative floating in the Bay of Campeche in approximately twenty-five meters of water. Cause of death: exsanguination from laceration of aorta; fishing harpoon puncture. Killer unknown.

Leine threw the file to the ground and sprang to her feet, backing away from it as if it were on fire.

I killed Carlos.

But you didn't know it was him, a voice inside her said.

Doesn't matter. I killed him, another voice screamed.

Yes, it does. You know what you need to do. He sent you to kill him. He knew.

He KNEW.

Clenching her fists and breathing fast, her heart hammered inside her chest as blinding, hot rage formed in her belly and rose, coursing through her.

"Game. Over."

Leine sprinted across the open lawn, coming to rest at the base of the kitchen window. She'd disabled Eric's security cameras, an easy task since she'd installed them. The weight of Carlos's gun grounded her, reminding her why she was there.

An appropriate choice of weapon for what she was about to do.

Dishes clanked together inside the house, telling her Eric was tidying up after dinner. He had a housekeeper but usually sent her home before dinner, preferring to have his nights to himself. A creature of habit, Eric would then retire to his study to look over current security briefings.

Keeping to the shadows and using the surrounding shrubbery, Leine continued around the stately home, the sound of waves lashing the beach below. Lucky for her, Eric preferred to live far from his neighbors.

No one would hear a thing.

She reached the back patio and stopped near a large hydrangea bush. Light shone from the windows of Eric's study. The room was empty. Leine made her way to the pair of French doors that led inside.

They were locked.

She pulled out a set of picks she'd found in Carlos's apartment and had the door open in less than a minute. She'd gone back to get his car and to pick up another magazine for the 9mm, and figured they'd come in handy.

Easing the door open, she slipped inside the study, moved past the massive wooden desk, and sat down in a wingback chair opposite the fireplace.

CHAPTER 19

LEINE TURNED TOWARD the sound of footsteps padding down the hallway, and trained the gun on a point just inside the door. Eric walked into the room, head down as he paged through the file in his hands.

"Eric."

He froze mid-step. Leine rose from her chair and walked toward him.

"Leine." The wariness in Eric's voice was telling.

She circled him, sure to keep enough distance as well as block his access to the desk. True, he didn't work in the field, but that didn't mean there wasn't a gun in his desk drawer.

"Surprised to see me?" she asked, stopping directly opposite his position.

"Not really." The set of his shoulders told her otherwise.

"No? But what about those two men you sent after me in Amsterdam? I'll bet you thought they succeeded, didn't you? Really, Eric. You should know better than to use thugs like that. They weren't very imaginative."

"I don't know what you're talking about. What men?" The tiny flicker of his eyelid gave him away. She wouldn't have caught the slip if she hadn't known him so well.

"Cut the bullshit. I know you've been trying to kill me since Glushenko. I assume the bombing at the café was supposed to finish me off, along with the Frenchman, right? I'm surprised you left such an important job to an inexperienced kid. Or did you think Volkov would do the honors himself?" Leine narrowed her eyes as a flame of anger ignited in her chest, its intensity all but consuming her. Not killing him instantly took every ounce of control she had.

Let's see how he tries to slither out of this one.

Eric remained silent. He watched her, giving the impression that he was calculating his odds. She could almost hear his thoughts—she hadn't killed him yet. Maybe there was a chance to talk his way out of it. Or get to a gun.

You just keep thinking that, Eric. All the way to your grave.

His expression changed slightly, and his shoulders inched lower. He sighed before he spoke, as though he thought he might as well confess.

"When I didn't hear from you, I assumed you were dead. I sent Grant and Rogers to collect your things. I never gave the order to kill you."

"You're a shitty liar, Eric. Always have been."

"I'm not lying. Your account went inactive. I—"

"Ah yes. My account. I assume you're referring to the tracking program on my phone. Just when did you install *that* little device?" Leine was itching to squeeze the trigger. *Answers first, Leine.*

"A few months ago. It's an agency-wide procedure I recently implemented, so don't go off half-cocked." He nodded toward the gun.

"Oh, don't worry. I rarely do anything halfway." *I could just shoot him and leave. Why not?* She raised the gun.

Eric's eyes darkened and he clenched his fists. "What the hell do you want?"

"Why have you been trying to kill me?"

"I haven't." Something flashed behind his eyes.

Leine moved quickly, feinting left with her cast as she swept her leg behind him and threw him to the floor. He landed on his side with a grunt, and she flipped him onto his chest. With her knee in his back and her cast against his neck, she shoved the 9mm into the back of his head.

"I see you've been keeping up with your martial arts training," he quipped, his words muffled by the thick carpeting.

"Isn't that just like you? Make a joke when you're on the losing end of the equation." Leine leaned in, putting more pressure on his neck. "How could you send me to kill Carlos?" She grimaced at the crack in her voice. *Don't lose it now, Leine.*

"I needed the best operative for the job."

"Fuck you." Memories cascaded through her mind of Carlos floating in the black sea, a spear—the spear she'd used to kill him—sticking out of his chest, a trail of blood streaming from the wound. She felt as though someone had reached in and ripped out her beating heart. Tears streamed down her cheeks as she fought through the torment.

Carlos is gone. You can't bring him back, but you can avenge his death. Kill Eric. Now.

Leine blinked away the tears and aimed the gun, barely registering the deep intake of breath near the doorway.

"Mom? What are you *doing*?" Eyes wide and her mouth agape, April stared at them in horror. Tears welled in her eyes.

"April?" Confused, Leine looked from her daughter to Eric and back again. She pushed to her feet and backed away from both of them, still aiming the gun at Eric. She couldn't kill a man in front of her daughter. Especially her father, whether she knew it or not.

"What the hell are you doing with my daughter?" Leine demanded.

"What are *you* doing to Uncle Eric?" April ran to help him up. Eric climbed to his hands and knees and rotated his head, stretching his neck.

"Are you going to tell her or should I?" Eric asked, allowing April to guide him to a chair near the desk.

"Tell me what?" April asked, the pink in her cheeks deepening as she looked from one to the other.

"Your mother is a killer, April. She killed your Uncle Carlos."

"She what?" Disbelief flickered in her eyes as she turned to look at her mother. Leine's tenuous hold on her emotions shattered at the pleading in her daughter's expression.

"Don't listen to him, April. He's trying to blackmail me."

April glanced at Eric, doubt replacing a portion of the disbelief. "Is she telling the truth?"

Eric shook his head and gave her a sympathetic look. "Honey, she's been lying to you all along. For years."

"April, don't—"

April held up her hand and asked Eric, "Did she kill Carlos?" Her voice wavered.

"I'm afraid so." Eric looked at Leine, triumph gleaming in his eyes.

"No. She couldn't have. She—she loved him." Her anguish obvious, April turned to her mother. "Didn't you?"

"More than you can ever imagine," Leine said, her voice quiet. She closed her eyes. She'd never lied to April before. She couldn't start now.

"Your Uncle Eric sent me to—kill him. But he tricked me and told me it was someone else." There. It was done. She'd just admitted to her daughter that she was a killer. Let the chips fall where they may.

April stepped closer to Eric, conflicting emotions vying for dominance on her young face.

"She's lying, April," he said. "She knew it was him."

"You mean—" Panicked, April backed toward the door. "You're her boss. That means that you're as much a part of this as she is."

"Aw, honey, no. That's not how this works." Eric raised his hands, a sad smile on his face. Leine would have killed him then and there if April hadn't been in the room.

"Then how *does* it work?" April shook her head. "No," she whispered, tears streaming down her face. "You're *monsters*. I hate you both," she cried and ran from the room.

A gaping silence filled the hole where April had been standing. The urge to run after her was strong, but Leine stayed where she was. She wouldn't put anything past Eric. *He wouldn't hesitate to kill me if he had the chance, whether April was here or not.*

"Still going to kill me?" Eric asked, flicking imaginary dust off his trousers.

Leine ignored the question. "What is April doing here?"

"I thought it best that someone she knew and trusted was nearby when she learned the news of her mother's death." He shrugged. "Either way, I doubt she'll want to live with you now."

"You're not in any position to dictate where she lives or doesn't live. She and I will get through this, somehow."

"Oh? And what do you mean by that?" he asked, a smug look on his face. "I've already begun paternity testing. I'm pretty sure the judge will see things my way when I tell him what you do for a living. April will be much better off with me."

"You forget—April is old enough to have a choice, and besides, you'd expose your role in the Agency. I don't think a judge would want either of us raising her."

"Ah, but you forget, too. I know people, Leine."

That was true. Eric had an entire network of judges who owed him favors. But she still had one last card to play.

"What about the information Carlos discovered?" Leine asked. Eric stiffened. "Turns out, he found quite a bit of material on your off-book dealings. Especially with a well-known black market arms dealer named Adrian Volkov. And yes, there are photos. I doubt the vice president will be happy when he learns about your dealings with such a notorious criminal. If I were a betting woman, I'd say he'll want to know where all that money went. You know, since the Agency's essentially funded by the taxpayers and all." Not only that, but if he was found guilty of running his operatives as guns for hire, he'd do hard time.

She had to hand it to Eric, he kept his face impassive. The only tell she could see was a slight twitch in that same eyelid.

"So. It appears we're at an impasse." Eric steepled his fingers as he thought. "I could assume you're bluffing, that Carlos only mentioned his suspicions rather than giving you proof."

Leine reached inside her jacket, withdrew the CD from Carlos's locker, and tossed it on the desk.

"There's proof."

"Okay. Let's say you're telling the truth and that CD contains your so-called evidence of these alleged dealings. How do I know that once you're gone you won't hand a copy over to Henderson?"

"You don't. But I'll give you my word the information stays with me as long as you agree to three conditions."

"I'm listening."

"Condition one: I no longer work for you or the Agency. I'm out, Eric. I hate what I've become, and I hate you."

"Hate's such a strong word."

"Not nearly strong enough." *What are you doing, Leine? Kill him. April will forgive you, someday.*

No, she won't. And she'd never withstand police questioning once they found Eric's body. I'll go to prison for murder, and she'll be handed over to Social Services.

"Condition two: You never divulge to anyone that you're April's father, including April. And, that you never, ever attempt to take her from me."

"Go on."

"Three: you scrub my past so clean it would take an army of forensic investigators and IT specialists to figure out who I am and what I've done."

It was a good deal and he knew it. He'd be safe, at least for now, and he wouldn't have to have Leine killed or raise April, both of which were problematic. Raising a daughter wasn't easy, and the operatives he'd send to kill Leine would be loose ends, which he rarely left. Even so, Leine wasn't fool enough to believe she could live without looking over her shoulder.

"Well?" she asked.

"Deal." He held out his hand. Leine ignored him and strode to the door.

"And don't think that killing me will save you. I've made sure that in the event of my death all materials in a certain safety deposit box are to be sent directly to your boss, as well as to a reporter I know who works for a reputable news agency."

With that, Leine walked out the door to find her daughter.

CHAPTER 20

April 2007—Manarola, Italy

POWERFUL WAVES CRASHED against the rocks below her as Leine sipped a glass of the local white wine. She was seated alone at a small table in an idyllic outdoor café overlooking the Mediterranean. A gentle breeze played with a lush stand of bougainvillea climbing up the nearby wall of the restaurant, and brilliant sunlight danced across water an unimaginable shade of turquoise. People here laughed often and spoke in lyrical languages like Italian, Portuguese, and French. It had the rhythm and flow of a life, and Leine needed life after so much death.

She missed her daughter, wanted her to experience this place that she loved. She and Carlos had visited the Cinque Terre often together, and she'd come this time in the hopes of exorcizing those demons that plagued her sleep. But her daughter refused to come.

And the tequila wasn't working anymore.

The waiter stopped to take her order. Leine asked for the fresh fish of the day and another glass of wine.

It had been over four months since the night April discovered Leine's unforgiveable sin of killing Carlos. Their relationship, though civil, wasn't anything like what it had been before. April preferred to stay at Marta and James's place in Santa Rosa and grudgingly came home on the weekends. Whenever Leine managed a conversation with her, she wouldn't show any emotion at all. It had gotten to the point where Leine would have welcomed anger or rage, or a psychotic break. Anything but the cool indifference of the stranger with whom she now lived.

Leine hadn't worked in those four and a half months, had wanted to be there for her daughter and tried to make amends, but she couldn't break through the solid wall April had built around her emotions. Fortunately, Leine's investments and savings were such that she didn't have to work, at least for several years. And, in an odd twist of fate, Carlos had willed his estate to her. The thought of benefitting from his death made her ill, and she put all of his holdings into a trust to be paid out when April turned eighteen.

The nightmares were getting worse now, and she rarely slept. Her grief at losing Carlos was still raw and seemingly insurmountable, so she fled her home and her indifferent daughter to come to the place she loved most.

A shadow crossed her table and, shielding her eyes, she looked up. A man's silhouette blocked the sun, and Leine squinted at him, trying to get a better look.

"I'm sorry, but I was admiring the view and was wondering if you'd like some company."

American accent. Nice cologne. She nodded, and replied, "I'm not much company, I'm afraid."

He sat next to her and smiled. In his mid to late thirties, he had dark, wavy hair, nice, white teeth, and a pair of friendly brown eyes.

"That's all right. Neither am I." He turned his face toward the sun. His prominent chin and nose made her think Italian-American or possibly Greek.

"What's a beautiful woman like you doing by yourself in a place like this?" His smile softened the lame, well-used line, and she smiled back. There was something calming about him.

"I lost someone very close to me, and I'm here to see if I can feel again. And you?" No use beating around the bush. It wasn't like she was looking for someone. After what she'd done for a living, what man would want to be with her? The only person who'd be even remotely interested would have to have done the same kind of work as she did. Leine wasn't interested in an assassin dating service. She was out of that life for good.

He nodded. "Sorry to hear that. I'm here on family business. My name's Frank, by the way," he said, extending his hand.

Leine smiled as she shook it. "Leine."

The waiter came with the drink Leine had ordered, and Frank asked for a glass of the local wine, as well. They sat in companionable silence until the waiter returned, and they toasted each other and watched the sunset. When her dinner came, Frank regaled her with stories of business deals gone bad and shady characters, giving her the impression he might have been connected in the criminal sense.

Well, why the hell not? She'd had a few glasses of wine and Frank was attractive. A member of the mafia would be par for the course. Her previous profession wouldn't scare him off. Besides, she didn't deserve an upstanding member of society. Not after what she'd done.

After dinner, they weaved their way along the winding streets of the town, stopping at a small bar for a nightcap. When Leine mentioned it was time for her to go, Frank insisted he be a gentleman and walk her back to her room.

"You must not be from the States," Leine said, laughing. "Your manners are showing."

"Actually, I live in LA. And you?"

"San Francisco," she replied.

"Well, now, that sounds like a match made in heaven, if you ask me. Same coast, but different cities. What's not to like?"

He walked her to her door, and she turned to kiss him. He wrapped his arms around her and she leaned into his embrace. Months without human contact rose to the surface, but she stifled the urge to ask him to stay. Leine took a step back.

"I should go." She slid the key in the lock and opened the door.

"Can I see you tomorrow?"

Leine smiled. "Why not?" She turned to go inside.

Frank placed his hand on her arm. "Hey, I never got your last name."

"You're right, you didn't."

Frank grinned, took a step back, and put up his hands. "Okay, I get it. You're an enigma wrapped in a shawl, or something like that. Well, my last name is Basso."

Frank Basso, she thought as she closed the door. *It's got a nice ring to it.*

THE END

Other books by D.V. Berkom:
LEINE BASSO THRILLER SERIES:
Serial Date
Bad Traffick
The Body Market
Cargo
The Last Deception
Dark Return
Absolution
Dakota Burn

KATE JONES THRILLER SERIES:
Kate Jones Thriller Series Vol. 1 *(Books 1-4)*
The first four novellas in the Kate Jones Thriller Series: *Bad Spirits, Dead of Winter, Death Rites,* and *Touring for Death.*
Cruising for Death
Yucatán Dead
A One Way Ticket to Dead
Vigilante Dead

Continue reading for an excerpt from the Leine Basso Thriller SERIAL DATE:

CHAPTER 1

PETER BRONKOWSKI PEELED himself away from the prop closet. He needed air. The onlookers parted to give him space.

Oh my God, oh my God, they're going to shut us down. When this gets out the motherfuckers are going to crucify me. All the hard work, the hustling, the endless lunches listening to that blowhard Senator Runyon, all of it would be for nothing. Peter shook his head to clear it. His breath came out in fast gasps, threatening to hyperventilate.

At first, Peter thought it was a grotesque looking mannequin with fake blood stains down the front and side of its torso. The moment reality clicked, a jolt of shock split him, pooled behind his eyes and slid to his gut. With dawning comprehension, Peter realized the blood was real. And it was no mannequin.

It was Mandy.

Peter turned back to the prop closet. Everyone stared at him, as if he had the slightest idea what to do now. Fuck. He couldn't see a way out of this. Too many people had seen the body. He thought of his brother, Edward, but brushed the idea away.

Mandy was dead. Murdered. Sweet, small-town-sexy Mandy. *Who would want to kill her?* Now Tina, yeah, he could sort of see that, she could be quite the bitch. But Mandy? And which one of the cons did it? No getting around it, he'd have to call LAPD. They'd be swarming all over the place. Better find another home for Edward. He wasn't going to like that one bit. Edward didn't do well with change.

Gene Dorfenberger walked toward him, pushing people out of his way.

"Give him some room! The man can't think with you crowding him like that." Reluctantly, the small crowd began to disperse, a few stealing one last look at the gruesome sight.

Gene glanced at Mandy's body and shook his head. "Now why would somebody go and cut off her arm?" He edged closer, squatting to take a better look. "And an ear? What kind of sick fuck would do that?"

Peter froze. "Her ear's missing?"

"Yeah."

Peter shook his head to clear it. *It can't be.* He took a deep breath to try to stop the dizziness. Everything was spiraling out of control.

Originally slated as low-cost filler for summer, Serial Date had turned into the most watched reality show on television. Less than a year and a half ago he couldn't get the mailroom clerks to return his calls much less the now regular invitations to private parties and dinners with the network brass. They all wanted a piece and Peter had happily parlayed the lust for the extraordinary profits generated by the show into extra bargaining power.

This is it. It's over. We'll never recover.

"It's going to be rough. You're going to have to do some major damage control." Gene's sharp gaze traveled from the massive amount of blood soaked into the costumes scattered around Mandy back to Peter.

Peter nodded, his expression grim. "We've got to get somebody legit in here so the cops'll think we're taking steps to keep the contestants safe."

If Gene took offense at the comment, he didn't show it. "I think I know just the person. It'll take some doing, but I hear she's strapped for cash."

Peter looked at Gene with disbelief. "She? Gene, we need somebody who'll keep the fucking cops at bay, not another broad on the set."

Gene shook his head. "Oh, this one ain't just another broad, believe me."

CHAPTER 2

LEINE BASSO DROPPED her purse on the floor, kicked off her shoes and stalked across her apartment to the kitchen. She opened the refrigerator door and grabbed a beer. The old appliance clanked in protest.

Holding the cool bottle to her forehead, she walked over to the couch and dropped onto it, sighing with relief. Three down, two to go. God, she hated looking for a job. Especially when it seemed like everyone and their brother was out there doing the same thing.

Leine set the bottle on the thrift-store maple coffee table, leaned back and hiked up her skirt, struggling to peel off her pantyhose. It wasn't easy. The oppressive heat and the high humidity was fairly unusual for Seattle, even if it was the middle of August. Didn't matter if she took a shower or not; once she stepped outside, she was as damp as if she had.

Why didn't I just stay at the last job? Leine paused for a moment in her battle for freedom from the polyester and nylon blend. *Oh yeah. Because you didn't like the creep masquerading as your boss and he ended up on the floor with a broken collar bone when he tried to grope you.* A real player. Not only that, but he was a few heads shorter than Leine's five-foot-ten inches and she knew from experience that the guy would continue to be on her ass, one way or another, in order to prove himself the alpha dog. A lot of short guys had a chip on their shoulder. Except her husband, Frank.

Correction: her ex-husband.

The marriage hadn't exactly worked out. She made it four years.

Giving up on her stockings for the moment, she crab-walked back into the kitchen, opened the freezer and stuck her head in. Too bad her whole body didn't fit. Between the sound of her breathing and the death rattle of the fridge, she barely heard her cell phone go off.

She backed out and shut the freezer door, stuck her hand in her purse and grabbed her phone.

"Leine Basso."

"Leine? It's Gene Dorfenberger."

That was a blast from the past. *Why would Gene be calling her?*

"Hey, Gene. It's been a while."

"Yeah. Hey I got a line on a sweet job that you'd be perfect for. The only thing is, it starts right away and it's in L.A. You available?"

L.A. Not her first choice. Too many memories and they weren't happy.

"Depends on the job, Gene. I'm not freelancing anymore."

"No, no, nothing like that. See, I work for this guy named Peter Bronkowski. He's got a small problem and I was thinking you could fix it for him. He needs some special protection for his TV show. Ever heard of Serial Date?"

"I never watch television." Leine walked back to the freezer and stuck her head inside again.

Crappy airless one bedroom apartment.

"Oh. Well, it's this gigantic hit reality show that uses ex-cons as dates for really hot looking women, only the guys are billed as serial killers."

"This is a hit show?" Last time she had a TV, she emptied her gun into it after watching a sitcom. Apparently, she hadn't missed much.

"Yeah, the biggest. Anyway, one of the contestants was killed and ..."

Leine brought her head up, barely missing the edge of the old Hotpoint. "How do you know she was killed?"

"Pretty obvious. I don't know of anybody who'd cut off their own arm and ear before killing themselves. Van Gogh she ain't."

"Any ideas who might've done it? I mean, you've got how many ex-cons on the set? Did you check their records to see which ones did time for violent crimes?" Had the world gone crazy while she wasn't looking? Employing ex-cons wasn't usually a big deal, but putting them in close proximity to a bunch of beautiful women and having them act like serial killers made no sense at all.

"Not yet. Peter's delaying the call to the police until I talk to. What do you think? Interesting?"

Interesting wasn't the word.

"Why me? Why not some off-duty cop or something?"

"Because I trust you. I don't trust anybody else when it comes to family."

"What do you mean?"

"You remember my sister, Ella?"

Leine remembered that Gene was holy-shit-scared of Ella, with good cause. A fierce lady, she didn't take kindly to Gene's bullshit. He had the scars to prove it.

"Ella's kid's working on set as a gopher and I can't keep an eye on her all the time. I figured with the two of us we'd be able to make sure she stayed safe."

"So you think the killer's still hanging out on the set?"

"I don't know. Nobody has a clue, but obviously there are a lot of suspects. I'd feel better if you were here to back me up."

"How much and how long?"

"Peter said to offer you two large a week if you could start right away. It runs until they find who did it, maybe longer."

Two-thousand a week was a hell of a lot better than what she made now, which was nothing. And it's not like it would be a tough gig. She could probably get used to L.A. again. Mainly, she didn't like the people and she knew how to avoid people.

"I'll take it."

END EXCERPT

54051158R00102

Made in the USA
Middletown, DE
12 July 2019